Claire Fitzpatrick is an author of speculative fiction and non-fiction. She won the 2017 Rocky Wood Award for Non-Fiction and Criticism. Called 'Australia's Queen of Body Horror' and 'Australia's Body Horror Specialist', she enjoys writing about anatomy and the darker sides of humanity. She eats the skin of kiwifruit and likes to take notes about people on the train. She lives in Brisbane.

METAMORPHOSIS

A Collection of Short Stories

By Claire Fitzpatrick

Metamorphosis

ISBN-13: 978-1-925956-08-5

V1.0

Stories publishing history at the end of this book.

Printed in Palatino Linotype and Signo.

IFWG Publishing International
Melbourne

www.ifwgpublishing.com

For Isobelle

And

To my family, obviously.

Thanks for teaching me how to read, Mum. Too bad the terrible school didn't. Or maybe I was terrible? I don't know. In any case, look everyone, I can read and write!

Hey Dad! Thanks for the barbecues and the chats about space.

You know what? My family don't read my stories, so if someone doesn't tell them about this dedication, they'll never know.

And

To Matt, with love.

Also, I'd like to thank Wellington Point State High School. I stole about a dozen Sonya Hartnett books, which were great inspiration. I still have them and you're never getting them back.

Introduction

Recently I read over my stories and concluded that the woman who wrote them is inside me no longer. Some were written and published many years ago, some only recently. When I look at these stories I see the writer who died with me long ago; I see the writer I no longer recognise. It was not a bitter death—I can still recapture some of the thoughts I had while writing them. I can still see the neurotic thoughts I once had swimming in my mind. But I can no longer pluck them out and look at them, for they are simply not there.

Many of the ideas of these stories come from my personal experiences with Epilepsy and Borderline Personality Disorder. I am a crazy person who has seizures. Many of my ideas stem from my fears, my neurotic thoughts, my paranoia. The good thing about these thoughts is that I can transform them into something positive, and I can forget, for a while, my irrational idea that people follow me down the street. I don't like having Epilepsy, nor do I like having Borderline Personality Disorder, but I can't help but thank them. If they were not in my life magazine editors would not call me 'Australia's body horror specialist' and Australia's queen of body horror.' I would not have won the 2017 Rocky Wood Award for Non-Fiction and Criticism. I would not be a panellist at conventions. Life is a curious invention.

Why 'Metamorphosis'? I am sceptical, reclusive, afraid of the world, and of myself. I hate crowds. I think people are watching me. But I am not averse to people. I love them just as much as I fear and detest them. I like to take notes about them on the train. I like to imagine pulling people apart to understand them more. Maybe one day I'll learn to be a person like everyone else. As Charles

Bukowski once said, 'I don't hate people…I just feel better when they're not around.' These stories are speculative fiction. Some err into the realm of science fiction, others towards paranormal. Some are suspense, others are body horror. One thing is for certain—all of them are written by a paranoid author.

I don't know if people read my stories. I don't know if my work will survive the passing of time. I doubt any author can know for certain. What I do know is that *some* people read and like them enough to publish them. You can make anything up with words. Stories make you dip your toes into life more than once. Stories make you confront your intense fears and obsessions. While I may feel unreal at times, my stories are very much alive. Writers tell lies, but most of my stories have elements of truth within them. I am not deceptive by nature. I am not the most honest person in the world. However, perhaps the only way to get to know me is through my writing? Maybe. I still don't know who I am. But who does?

August 2018.

Table of Contents

Madeline..11
Eat...17
Mechanical Garden................................25
The Jacaranda House............................39
Transplant..49
The Eagle..63
Scarab...81
Senses...89
The Dog...99
The Town Hall......................................107
Metamorphosis.....................................115
Happy Birthday, Ebony.......................125
Synthetic...137
Andromeda..145
The Perfect Son....................................163
Thorne House.......................................173
Deep-Sea Fishing.................................177

Story Publishing History.....................197

MADELINE

Madeline peeled the first flake of skin from her thigh the day she turned fifteen. She had experienced the onset of puberty two years earlier — the sudden growth of hair under her arms and between her legs, the swelling of her breasts, the skin on her thin thighs growing thicker — and so assumed the peeling away of flesh was a natural, albeit slower, progression into womanhood.

A year later, she stood in front of the mirror and inspected her new sweet sixteenth birthday body, running her hands along the softness of her inner thigh, her fingers drawing circles on the darker areas where her legs rubbed together when she ran. She ran her palms over the back of her thighs, as a proper woman would feel around for cancerous lumps the day before an overdue check up at the doctors and froze when her fingers ran across an unusually hardened piece of flesh.

The strip of flesh came away like a Band-Aid, was roughly the thickness of a twenty-cent coin, and rectangular in shape. She stared at it curiously in her hand, running a finger across it, and she frowned. Her mind likened it to the strips of beef jerky her father always carried with him in his leather pouch when he worked on the farm. She gingerly brought it to her nose and sniffed, instantly recoiling as the pungent scent of unwashed feet and week-old food slammed into her nostrils. She flung the piece of flesh on the ground and took a step back, her heart thudding furiously against her chest.

She stared at the pink flesh, a stark contrast against the pristine white tiled floor, and wondered if her best friend Sally had a collection of her own skin, tied up in lavender rope and folded away in a neat little treasure chest. Sally had entered puberty early, at eleven years old, and had proudly worn strapless shirts and training bras that accentuated the flappy mounds of flesh that had affixed themselves to her thin, boyish body.

"I'm a woman now!" she had announced, excitedly. "I'm allowed to wear high heels."

Madeline wondered if she was supposed to mould the pieces of flesh to form breasts and strap them to her body with chunks of muscle. She had always been quite flat in that particular area. When all her friends wore bikinis, she would wear T-shirts and shorts, hiding away her lack of womanliness and femininity.

She dropped the strip of flesh on the bathroom floor and began to peel away more. The long, sinewy flanks on either side of her thighs came away with ease, as though she were pulling off chunks of hot, crispy flesh from a slow-roasted animal over a spit fire. The skin on the front of her thighs was entirely uncovered now, and she felt like a snake peeling away from its skin, except where its skin was scaly, hers was almost too soft, so tender it was almost like butter simmering on a hot stove. She imagined she was one of her father's bovines, butchered in the hot midday sun, her flesh quartered from top to bottom with a shiny silver meat saw, and suddenly she was hesitant as to what would happen next. Would she end up like them, rotting flesh too tough to be consumed, hide too rough to be of any use?

Madeline swallowed down a lump in her throat and froze as she heard the sounds of her mother rummaging around in the linen outside the bathroom. Heart thudding, she felt as though she was a deer trapped in the headlights. As the sounds died away, relief flooded her body and she relaxed, staring at her reflection in the grimy mirror.

Madeline felt as though her churning stomach was about to burst through her skin, blasting out like a cannonball and blowing a hole through the bathroom door. Her legs, usually steadfast in the uneasiness of bad situations, felt like jelly and ice cream mixed together, a trifle of wobbly knees and slippery feet, barely holding up her adolescent frame.

She stood in the middle of her mound of flesh and inspected her body in the mirror. Her mind wandered, and she realised why the human body was not built, neither bred, for its flesh to be consumed. To begin with, the anatomy and skeleton was all wrong. Her fleshy body, while oversized in some areas, did not have nearly as much flesh as a cow or a pig. And her shoulder blades and wide pelvis wouldn't cut as well as a lamb's. She also lived in an uncontrolled environment and ate whatever she fancied without even thinking about how it might affect the chewiness of her flesh. Humans contracted a range of infections, diseases, poisons, all of which multiplied with age. However, animals were slaughtered quite young, without ever obtaining the chance to sit around eating cheeseburgers and watching *Cheers* reruns.

Piece after piece, her flesh was expunged from her body, and in a matter of minutes Madeline had stripped away the meat from her feet, legs, stomach, arms, and hands. She imagined she was a butcher's subject, which he would later hang, bleed, behead, skin, gut, halve, and quarter. Maybe he would build an old-fashioned smokehouse with a stone fire pit, disposing of her offal and unwanted waste by burial, puree, or pulverisation. But humans weren't made to be eaten. She heard her mother curse and imagined her carefully folded linen tumbling out of the cupboard like a landslide.

Madeline gently palmed her chest, imaging herself on a runway, her voluptuous, yet lithe and attractive body showing off the latest Italian fashion trend. She closed her eyes and caressed her stomach, scrunching up the floppy folds of her tummy between her fingers. Slowly, she pulled away the lumpy flesh like string cheese, bits of blood and muscle cocooning themselves under her nails. Sacks of chubby adolescent fat fell away to join the flesh upon the floor, building up around her ankles. She felt as though she were standing on the hills of Machu Picchu, an ancient metropolis built not of stone but flesh, flesh of its ancestral inhabitants, of its long-lost worshippers singing praise as they cast unwanted souls down into the pits to meet their doom. She was now a proper woman, her body was her temple, and the torn away flesh revealed a most revered, ancient, womanly musculoskeletal structure to be praised by men who would dare to plunge themselves into her warm, meaty pit.

Her hand hovered near her sex, and she hesitated, as though to enter herself was an unspoken challenge. She paused and listened to the curses and insults at washing that refused to stay folded. Her mother had always been anal about things being uncooperative, and uncouth. What would she say about her daughter?

The folds around her entrance were velvety soft, yet feverishly moist, beckoning her fingers to come closer and claim their prize. She had touched herself, of course, as all girls did, starting off as a curious bystander, then became more adventurous, even conjuring up scenes of love and affection in her head. Now, at sixteen, she was ready to propel herself towards a new adventure, plunge herself into the depths of her very self. She slipped her fingers inside, then widened them, allowed room for the rest of her hand. Her teeth clenched, she reached for something to hold onto, and found something akin to a small stone, although fleshy and soft. She began to pull at it, and savagely ripped away, biting down on her tongue to hold back her cries of excruciation. Slumping to the floor in the mound of her own flesh, she held out her palm, and stared at the stone she had so painfully plucked.

"It's not a stone; it's a seed," she whispered in awe.

Hot blood tricked from between her legs and coated the muscle of her inner thighs, sliding down in between each fold of soft tissue and cell. She tossed it back and forth between her hands like a ball and marvelled at how light it was, yet how full and complete it felt as it rested on the ball of her palm. She wondered what the seed was doing inside her body, and how long it had been there for. Had it always been there, even as she was a child, or had it grown when she first began to bleed? What was it made of? It appeared to be some form of menstrual clot, yet harder, firmer, like a rock. What was its purpose? Had she just removed something that should have remained hidden within her body? Had she discovered a secret to womanhood that young women weren't supposed to know? And finally, since she was very sure it was a seed, where on earth was she to plant it?

Adolescence made no sense.

Madeline stared at herself in the mirror. Her reflection showed a beastly creature, a skinless, formless being without flesh. She reached her bony hand up to her head and pulled away her skullcap, then cracked open her skull, as easy as stripping away the fontanel during postnatal development, exposing her brain and the watery fluid it swam in. She had learned about the fontanel after her little sister had been born. It was surprising how calm she was when little Anne was born, and surprising how little tension she felt in her body now. She rolled the seed in her hand round and round, feeling its grainy substance, then she stopped, and moved her hand above her head.

She softly stroked her thoughts, surprised by how calm she was, how little tension she felt in her body.

"Am I seeing my true self? Is this what it means to be a woman? Is this how I learn the secrets of life?"

The seed slipped from her fingers without hesitation and dropped into the watery mess of her skull with a soft plop, minute drops of water flicking out over the sides of her head. She smiled as her head seemed to sew itself back together by mere thought, leaving behind the smallest trace of a line etched across her forehead.

She made quick work of pulling herself back together, rolling up two mounds of flesh to affix to her chest, moulding slabs of skin to add size to her hips, slapping on slivers of muscle to her thighs, sticking on clumps of fat to her buttocks. She scrubbed the blood away from her legs until she was fresh and clean, and admired the perfect juxtaposition of her face, how easy it had pulled together. She felt renewed, revitalised, and utterly beautiful.

She pictured herself walking down the street, head held high, heels clicking on the pavement, and envisioned the heads that would turn as she passed by potential admirers. How many handsome young men would ask her to dance? Would the other girls be jealous of her newfound womanhood? She imagined herself in the future, carrying a child on her womanly hips, smiling down at it fondly as it gurgled and cooed. Had her own mother once seen her in that light? Or had she always been the

15

demanding teen, shouting "I want, I want, I want!"?

Madeline took one last look at the mess on the floor.

"You did it, Madeline," she said, turning to look at herself in the mirror one last time. "You're finally a woman."

She slipped out of the bathroom and walked down the hall, smiling broadly with the confidence of her new self. Her mother was now in the kitchen and Madeline ran to her, wanting that motherly hug, that motherly love.

Instead, her mother screamed.

Eat

The meat hook was sturdy; the bloated carcass hung like clothes on a rack. Harlan pinched the skin on the man's back, digging the machete in firmly. He made a small incision, plunging his middle and index fingers from both hands into the opening. The skin peeled away easily, the back separating in two thick pieces. Harlan stripped the flesh from the legs and stretched the skin over the neck to the base of the skull. He snapped the ankles at the joints, bones breaking through the muscle and tendons. One foot came loose and broke off, sending sharp pincer-like shivers down Alex's spine. Harlan delivered one final blow, severing the head altogether, sending splatters of blood across his and Alex's faces.

"Is it…going to come back?"

Harlan said nothing. He lifted the skin away from the intestines, cracking the rib cage, breaking all the way down to the pelvis, the organs and intestines dripping out of the abdominal cavity.

"What if it comes back?"

"It's not coming back."

In the darkness around them, a blood-curdling cacophony reverberated around the building. The creaking of unoiled winches, the rattling of hooks and chains, and worse, the scratches and fists against the door, the groans and gargled screams of the Risen. Harlan looked at the corpse, drowning out the incoherent screams by his concentration on the task at hand.

They had taken shelter in Logonov Street, an old three-story Victorian house, built when the trams were still in use. Gaunt mango trees lined the overgrown garden, the trees unkempt, the mangoes left to rot. The curtains had been drawn, with newspaper plastered on every window. The house had been empty for many months. Ever since *They* returned. The furniture remained, covered by large plastic sheets. Harlan had left the row of plaster saints on the fireplace mantle.

"You don't want to slice up the colon or the bladder," Harlan muttered. "It's messy."

Alex's brows furrowed and bit down on her lower lip.

"When are we moving on, Harlan? We can't do this forever. The Council has eyes and ears everywhere." She shifted on her feet, nervously patting her brow with a stained handkerchief.

Harlan groaned. "The only way they'll find out is if you tell them, idiot. Now help me!"

Around them, the light jittered and flashed as the bare bulb swung violently, as though propelled by an invisible wind in the stale air. Cobwebs hung from the ceiling. Pieces of skin and sinew littered the ground where Harlan had dumped the unwanted flesh. Some were serrated, others cut off in large chunks, dripping with blood.

Harlan stabbed two wounds into the corpse's chest cavity, piercing through the soft membrane. With one swift move he ruptured the diaphragm, causing his innards to burst out of his abdominal cavity and pool at his feet. He stuck out his index and middle finger, and with one steady motion, pressed them together as the organs and intestines exploded out of the man.

"What if it *does* come back?"

"It's not coming back!" Harlan snapped. "Listen. The scientists, the physicians…they're all saying mass hysteria. But these things…they're the playthings of witch doctors. They're something else."

Alex sighed. They were everywhere: rotting masses of insect-infested flesh, movements slower than the stupor of drunken men. Yet they were persistent, their tenacity and superior strength beyond any human's. Before they'd found the safe house, Alex thought it was comical, in a way. They appeared shrewd, conjuring up mini genocides in small towns, their stuttering footsteps reverberating around the streets as terrifying as loads of gunfire. They just kept coming, and nobody knew how to stop them.

"I'm going to open him up."

Harlan kicked the corpse's head across the room. A shadow passed over the window, obscuring the light from the slowly setting sun. He held up the machete, the blood-coated metal sheen reflecting the sweaty lacquer of the rotting body. A rumble of thunder cascaded across the sky, and a flow of fetid liquids gushed from the deep thoracic chasm as Harlan plunged the machete into the corpse's chest. The scent of rotting flesh filled the room. Alex rubbed her hands together, imagining the grittiness of the corpse's bodily fluids under her fingernails, inhaling the scent of an animal cadaver permeating the air, tasting the saltiness of an open wound on her tongue. Dry-swallowing, she filled her mouth with saliva to wash away the foul taste, but nothing she did could alleviate the sensation; the taste of death remained. Gasping, Alex stepped backwards, poised to pounce. Her breath came out in short, ragged intervals. She could not control her body. It trembled, yet she remained standing, frozen.

"I think we should go..."

Harlan groaned, rubbing his forehead in exasperation. "You want to eat, don't you?" he snapped, turning to face her. "Or do you want to starve?" He grabbed her by the shoulders, shaking her firmly, his eyes wide in a crazed rage. "I don't want this any more than you do, but what are we to do, huh? I'm starving, Alex."

A muffled burst of gunshots echoed outside the house, piercing the cacophony of rallying cries and shrill screams. Harlan was surprised anyone was idiotic enough to leave their safe houses. The air raids usually kept people indoors, yet rations were scarce, and there were only so many days most could remain cooped up in their boarded-up houses before turning the guns on themselves. Alex worried Harlan would view his gun not as a weapon but as an eternal saviour.

"Look. We need a plan. We can't stay here. We can't eat this thing. Who knows what it will do to us? Maybe we'll catch the virus?"

Harlan shook his head erratically. "No! I heard it's fine. If it doesn't bite us, if their saliva doesn't touch our skin, we're okay."

Alex and Harlan both looked at the bloated body, slowly swinging on the meat hook in the cool evening breeze. Harlan stepped forward. Alex hesitated. The corpse wore garments elaborately constructed to marry with its flesh, laced through skin like a corset, hooked into bone. Its neck, devoid of a head, appeared the remains of an unfortunate vivisection, exposed vertebra sharpened to points, the scent of sweat rising hotly from its body like volcanic steam.

"You first."

Alex bit down on her bottom lip, running her tongue along her teeth. Her stomach knotted endlessly inside her body, twisting and turning like a knife wound to the gullet. Once They'd returned, looting became almost second nature, yet all they had found were scraps. Not even the churches were spared of their treasures. She'd watched a priest shovel sacramental bread into his mouth like there was no tomorrow. For all Alex knew, there wasn't. She looked at Harlan, then at the corpse, then at the pile of flesh sitting at its feet. Slowly, she bent down, and sat on her haunches, staring at the foul remains of what was once a human person. It smelled of mildew and overripe fruit. Its cruel, razor-thin lips were clammy, as grey as its crumbling, pestilential skin. She thought of the corpse when they'd found it, masticating on innards, its guttural voice moaning as its teeth tore out chunks of flesh from a young boy's throat. Now, the tables had turned.

"I...can't, Harlan."

"God damn it, Alex!"

With a vicious force, Harlan grabbed the back of her neck and pushed her face towards the body. He knelt beside her, machete to her neck, his eyes as crazed as the corpse's, pressing his lips to her ear.

"If you don't eat, I'm going to ravage you," he whispered, "I'm going to feast on every inch of your skin. On every curve of your body." He ran his hands over her head, over her forehead, over her cheeks, and placed both hands on the back of her neck. He pressed his thumbs into her throat, holding her tightly in place.

"You don't deserve to live."

The gunshots rang louder. Alex wrangled her hands around Harlan and pulled herself from his grasp, racing over to the window. Below, a large group of Returned congregated outside the front door, shambling against one another, stumbling, some chewing on pieces of meat and viscera.

"God!"

Harlan raised the machete. "Come back here!"

Alex sprinted out of the room. Outside was a long corridor leading to a smaller room, and a short staircase sitting against the wall, pausing at a platform before winding downwards. Alex knew climbing the stairs would only lead her closer to her eventual death. Still, her eyes lingered on the doorway, and the corpse lying face down in the hall. Slowly, it pushed itself up from the burgundy hall runner, its rotting legs stretched back, what remained of its thighs and feet pushed firmly into the floor. The corpse's decaying ribs jutted forward; its neck bent to the side at an impossible angle. It opened its mouth. Screaming, Alex leapt backwards, cannoning into Harlan. He wrapped his arms around her. A bubble of yellow, aqueous juices dripped from the cavity in the corpse's chest. Alex kicked her legs wildly in the air as Harlan lifted her from behind. He dragged her down the hall and back into the room, bumping into the hanging body.

"Let go of me! We'll both die!"

"You first!"

"Get off me!"

Harlan pressed the machete to her neck, his back to the body. Its pungent odour filled Alex's nostrils. Her insides twisted. Harlan hooked his thumb in her mouth, laughing.

"Come and get her!" he shouted.

The corpse appeared at the doorway, its jaw hanging open, its eyes vacant and gleaming in the dim light. It raised itself, twisted, blistered strands of flesh dripping from its flesh like melted cheese. Its body—a grotesquely misshapen husk, muscle and fat withered away, its arms swinging like wind chimes in a breeze—ambled forward robotically. Alex screamed.

"Please!" Alex kicked her legs, furiously twisting them to

21

escape Harlan's grasp. A passage of light fell on the corpse; its flesh glistened and pulsated, oozing droplets of blood and pus on the floor.

Alex whipped her head to the window, listening to the sounds of sirens and a commanding military-like speaking through a megaphone. Her heart raced as she waited for someone, anyone, to race up the stairs and save her. With all the force she had left in her body, she elbowed Harlan in the stomach and scrambled to her feet, racing over to the broken window. On the road below sat a battered green Ford cargo truck with an attached hay tray and gate littered with fetid bodies. A troop of army personnel leapt out of the truck.

"Hey! Up here! Help me!"

Alex bashed her fists against the broken window, sending shards of glass flying across the room. "Help me! Up here!"

"Get back here, you bitch." Harlan pulled at Alex's arm, dragging her into his embrace. He pinned her arms behind her back and slid his arms between them, pulling on her elbows. Wincing, she twisted her legs. The corpse stepped forward. Harlan pushed her closer. She was but a few steps away from the blood-slobbering beast. Alex dug her nails into her fists, her jaw tight. She pressed her teeth down over her lower lip, eyes furiously darting to the doorway.

Blood dripped from the remains of the hanging corpse, splashing into the small pool which had thickened below. Flies buzzed around the blood, dipping and diving amongst the waxen, decomposing flesh. Alex looked over her shoulder at the meat hook. The remains of the body dropped to the ground with a thud. Her body moved before she could think. She twisted out of Harlan's grasp, then clasped the meat hook and drove it through his neck. Gasping, she collapsed on the ground, eyes on the slowly approaching corpse.

Gunshots echoed in the hallway. The scent of gasoline filled her nose. She looked over her shoulder at her brother, blood bubbling in his mouth, and she stared at him, wanting to cement his defeated face within her mind one last time. With one last, sudden force, he wrapped his legs out around her waist and clung to her as tightly as he could, his blood soaking her clothes. His body went limp. The corpse stepped closer. It stretched out its arms as it came to a staggering halt two feet in front of her. She glanced at the empty hallway. The corpse lunged forward. Alex screamed.

MECHANICAL GARDEN

There is no life inside the void. No air, no water, no vegetation. But I'd been exhaustively prepared and equipped to survive. Had I not been, my mind would already be fragmenting, my bones incinerated to ash, and my very DNA shredded past the point that nobody and nothing could put me back together again. Even optimal preparation offers no sure protection to the psyche because the seductive alien reality of the void assaults the mind itself.

When I first enter, I see home. I don't know what the supervising camera mounted on my helmet shows, but dismal autumn leaves swirl erratically in wind I can't feel, like a puppet jerking spastically. The slope of the forest ridge looms over all; the dark, crumbly brush behind the utility shed hides a huge nest of vicious hornets; a dead olive tree in the front yard cradles contemplative ravens in its skeletal arms which watch with patient hunger.

And the house sits like a spider in the centre of it all. The house in which I was born, and where I'd always imagined I'd die. The house which bespeaks "home" in every crooked board and broken shutter.

Inside the void is a garden built for bones. A man-made garden, a Zen garden; however, the moss and the pruned trees and gravel are all made from clay, the flowers made from particularly designed pieces of flesh, the stems formed from gristle. This is a garden not for growing, but decay. Beside the garden is a small portable radio. On the ZF4 TM, they are playing a sonata written by a musically gifted monk for violin and cello, which sounds like claps of thunder. I am unsure of how to move my limbs. I feel listening to it should bring me pleasure, but all I feel is emptiness and claustrophobia.

It takes real discipline to close my eyes. However, I cross my legs and sit beside the garden anyway, feeling my face relax, my muscles loosen, my heart beating at a steady pace. *One, two, three, four… One, two, three, four… One, two, three, four… One, two, three, four.*

There may be no ocean inside the void, but I see it nonetheless. I see the veil of mist over the gully, the pink sky, the shaly yellow dam wall, and over the hills, the sea. The great, beautiful, terrifying mass of sea. There had been creatures back then. Night-seeing birds comfortably blind to my anxiety to escape. No moon, no stars; just the totality of darkness mingled with pink and my prickled skin, its elasticity evaporated, left unable to warn me of dangers. And fish, hordes of fish. Before, I'd travel with my father to catch the lamprey, the river monster able to swim upstream, away from its school, alone. The riverbed had been strewn with slippery boulders. If I slipped, I could have been forced down and pinned under the thundering water and quickly swept away. I wouldn't have been the first person to drown there. Dad had told me the only way to pick them off was to grab them by their mouths. But they congregated in a very deep crevice, and I wasn't too keen on losing my hand. The lamprey was a fish that couldn't be caught on a base, with a rod, on a line. But now, there are no more fish. And I don't think they'll ever come back.

I stand up and begin to pace the garden, fingers tapping against my sides. I think, in a few years, after I die, everything else will die, and it will all become mechanical. A mechanical garden. No flowers, no weeds, but derelict clusters of botanical imaginings. A toxic cave filled with dank air. I often wonder: what *is* a mechanism? Unlike the green idylls of neatly pruned rosebushes and the leafy plumes of dead branches, the mechanical garden will become an accumulation of waste, with a stale body of water weaving through rusted pipes, growing nothing.

I think of my mind. After my diagnoses, mother had told me our minds were machines. She had read about it, as she had never known anyone with Epilepsy.

"Our minds are essentially subject to the same laws of physics as any other machine," she'd said. "As soon as we understand those laws more fully and have a better idea of the micro-functional structure of the brain, we should be able to build machines which can equal or even exceed the human capacity for thinking." She'd smiled and ran her fingers through my hair as I leaned against her chest, wrapping my arms around her waist. "Maybe one day your Epilepsy will be cured. Maybe one no-one will have Epilepsy at all."

I drop to my haunches and tap my fingers on my helmet, and for a moment, I miss Mother. I miss her perfume. Her face floats in my mind like driftwood, and I hear her thin laughter echoing in my ears.

"Do you know how to protect yourself?" she'd asked. We'd been preparing for the evacuation, memorising our numbers, the times we had to be at our locations to be transported away. "I cannot believe we are leaving," she'd said, gesturing to the broken windows, the burning rubble, the overturned carts. "Where will we go? How could they be so reckless?"

I'd followed mother's gaze but could not imagine the town as it had once been. The destruction had been beautiful in a macabre sort of way. Once bustling with life, now empty, with rubbish and abandoned belongings littering the streets.

"Theft and starvation," she'd said, while teaching me how to load a shotgun, "anarchy. You mark my words. All hell will break loose. We must remain vigilant. Are you prepared, love?"

I'd nodded mutely. But it was a lie.

I sigh, my thoughts turning back to reality. I don't know if I will ever see mother again. The siren buzzes, and the sky window opens slowly. The drone looks little more than propellers and plastic, but its ability to self-stabilise, to hold a GPS-based position, and respond to questions with juvenile, but efficient, answers proves it has reached the level of autonomy that makes it an intelligent machine. I don't know who controls the drone; all I know is that my weekly food provisions and anticonvulsants arrive at the same time on the same day every week. It gives me a sense of routine, and something to look forward to.

"Hello Chippy," I say, pulling the food package from the drone. "How are you today?"

Chippy hums, hovering in the air in front of my face. I am both scared and impressed by its accuracy, as though it can see me sitting in the garden, waiting for it to arrive. Its chip tells the drone to maintain its height, and its GPS corrects its course when it flies out of range.

"Not in a talkative mood today, I see." I pull the package from Chippy and place it beside me. "I'm not feeling too loquacious myself. It hasn't been a very eventful day. Mrs Alexander keeps yelling at her husband for not hanging the washing." I smirk. "And Old Tom keeps mowing the lawn at five in the morning. Has he not a shred of care for anyone else? He's a crumbling, fumbling old fool."

Chippy says nothing.

"Fine, then. Be that way. See if I care."

I sigh. Time does not exist inside the void. My imagined neighbours cannot hear my cries for help.

I turn to the drone. It's been many weeks since I've asked it specific questions, and answers need updating.

"Why didn't anyone stop the power surge? Why didn't the UNSC-5 do anything to help?"

"The UNSC-5 erected a ten-kilometre exclusion zone. The UNSC-5 advised residents to leave the fallout hotspots. The UNSC-5 could not prevent Reactor Number 16539-1's power surge. The reactor was not encased in a containment vessel. The experimental procedure failed."

I roll my eyes. "You told me this before. Word for word. But I'm trapped here, alone. I need real answers. You don't understand the concept of being alone because you're not human. To be alone is…" I inhale deeply, holding back tears. "Before all this happened, I already felt alone. Epilepsy is a solitary condition. You withdraw from the world around you, afraid you'll embarrass yourself in front of people. To be alone because you are different is the ultimate punishment. And now…I am here, alone.' I sniffle and wipe away my tears, straightening my back. "You can't concoct ideas of being alone, feeling like you've already spent an eternity invisible within a room full of people, and being left to die, because you're not human." I wrap my arms around my waist. "What happens when someone comes to collect me? I need to be informed."

"No-one is coming to collect you for a very long time."

I frown and look over at the package. My hunger viciously claws at my stomach, but I can't submit. I need to keep the food as long as possible. There is no telling when more packages will enter the void, and I have to keep up my strength. I take out the anticonvulsants and quickly swallow two.

I sigh and cross my arms. "What happened to the emergency cooling system?"

"The cooling system was shut down following another power surge. It was deemed unnecessary to remain in operation, as it needed to stay heated to test the new voltage regulating system."

"What did it release?"

"There are multiple hypotheses," the drone replies. "Hydrogen, either produced by the overheated steam-zirconium reaction or by the reaction of red-hot graphite with steam which, together, produced hydrogen and carbon monoxide. Also, a thermal explosion of the reactor deemed a result of the uncontrollable escape of neutrons caused by the complete water loss in the reactor core."

I nod. This is not news to me. However, I had hoped the drone had been remotely updated by those able to offer more information, to shed more light on my situation within the void. While at first I had felt comfort and safety within the void, I now feel a sense of discomfort and confinement. The nuclear explosion. I had no idea of knowing what would be next, or if I'd survive. And, if I did, what kind of world I would be left with? Faces had flashed before my eyes. And your face, smiling sadly at me, yet alight with hope. Everyone had gone about their business, oblivious to the terror they were about to face. And then, one by one, people began coughing up buckets of blood and viscera, along with their lungs. Officials turned to the streets, shouting into megaphones, urging the citizens to leave.

"Attention! Attention all residents. Due to high levels of radiation

exposure, the High Council has ordered your immediate evacuation.

"For the attention of the residents of Gwayorm! Following the accident at the Halina Power Station in the city of Gwayorm, The Bluecoat Alliance, their officials, and all military forces are ordering residents to temporarily evacuate. This is not a drill. All citizens will be taken to the Tampa Research Facility Station in preparation for immediate evacuation. Please take all government and personal documents with you, as well as identification. If you have a medical condition, please report it to the supervising officer. I repeat: this is not a drill.

All homes will be guarded by officials during and after the evacuation period. Residents, be sure to turn off all electrical appliances within your homes before evacuation. Please remain calm and follow directions in an orderly manner in the process of this evacuation. Repeat: this is not a drill."

Sighing, I pick up the package. Freeze-dried meat and vegetables and dehydrated drinks. A small medical kit. And a variety of condiments: tomato sauce, mustard, salt, pepper, and a round container of mixed herbs. I stare at the package, my stomach now feeling empty.

"Do you remember the plan?" Mother had asked, two hours into the evacuation. Authorities had planned for compulsory resettlement should the need arise. But there had been stories of defectors seeking refuge in the Exclusion Zone, thirty kilometres from the town. The EZ was built to restrict access to hazardous areas, inside the town itself, but older people did not want to leave their homes. I imagined them comforted by wild dogs, wandering around the abandoned train tracks, the abandoned houses, living as comfortably as they could before their inevitable death.

"I'm scared," I'd murmured, stuffing clothing and important documents into a sports bag. *"Why can't I come with you? Why do I have to go somewhere else?"*

"Don't worry, pet," Mother had said, placing her hand on the small of my back. *"We'll be together soon. They're probably just making sure everyone who needs medication has access to it. Besides, they said we'll be back in a week or so. Don't take anything you don't need. Just your papers, the medication you have left, and other important documents."* You smiled and tapped my forehead, running your soft hand down my

skin, pausing to cup my face. "I love you."

"Stop thinking."

"Excuse me?" I turn to the machine and raise a dubious brow. "Stop thinking?"

"How else am I supposed to monitor you if you think so loudly?"

"Monitor me?"

"Yes. You didn't think you were really alone down here, did you?"

I feel the colour drain from my cheeks, and I turn away, puzzled, retreating once again into my thoughts. *Not alone? Who else is here?* Stomach churning, I wonder if perhaps I am not as alone as I thought.

I'd filled a glass of rust-tasting water and drank deeply, choking down the foul taste until I had emptied the cup. I'd placed the cup on the side of the sink, and it sat precariously, leaning towards the dirty kitchen linoleum. Before the evacuation, after my birthday, Mother had looked at me as I pushed the cup over, watching as it smashed against the ground. Then I'd walked outside to the veranda and sat down on the old cane chair, leaning back as far as it would allow. I'd closed my eyes, imagining a world where Epilepsy did not exist, where my body didn't betray me.

I shake my head, staring at the package in my hand. The food is tasteless, yet I eat it anyway. My own exclusion zone is the void. A beautiful punishment. This beautiful garden reminds me of the ugliness within me. Left within the confines of my own imagination with Chippy as my confidante, who I know is only here so talking to myself doesn't make me feel so crazy. I close my eyes. In my mind I can see the little bench under the olive tree, the pine and cypress trees, I can smell the sweetness of the air, and an unexpected rush of affection for my mother courses through my bones so suddenly I look up at the drone and huff out a sigh.

"Oh, Chippy. What would I do without you?"

"You would die."

I smirk. "You're only saying that, pal."

"Incorrect. I dispense your medication. You would die."

I imagine taking Chippy home with me, back to my real home, outside the void. "We could sit outside, overpowered by the night odours, but unmoving, as though we belonged to the land around us," I say. "It would not be shameful to be afraid. We would listen to the loud croaking of frogs; we would feel the uncomfortable intimacy of the cold as it weaves its way around our bones, stiffening our joints; we would sit together, wrapped up in the thick air, once suffocating, now a comfort. A comfort of being outside. A comfort of being amongst life."

"I have no capacity for intimacy, and you would not be alive."

"We'd go outside the house and breathe the fresh, cool air," I continue, now pacing around the garden. "I just want to breath cool air again." I sigh. "And the darkness would be so black, but it wouldn't be oppressive, it would be liberating. We'd smell eucalyptus and smoke. We'd sit together and reminisce about the past, about how we thought we'd not survive and how all our fears almost crushed us down into little pieces. And my family would be there, laughing as we enjoyed a meal together."

"You would be crushed down into little pieces."

"And then we'd laugh about it, laugh how crazy it was to assume one person could survive outside the void. How it was unfair for others to be plucked out of the world and thrown into the void without anyone asking if that's what they wanted," I say, gesticulating wildly into the air. "We'd watch as they'd slowly destroy each other, but then…it would be me who would be destroyed more than you, since you are mechanical, a machine inside a garden, a mechanical garden." I sigh. "Oh, you will never understand. You don't even know what social isolation feels like. The fear, the horror. Worrying whether a seizure would strike me down like lightning and I would die."

"On the contrary, I understand more than you think. I understand you are trapped here. I understand you were left here to die. People like you are useless. People like you cannot be put to work. People like you cannot be released back into the population because you are a hindrance. You do not exist."

"You don't understand anything, you stupid robot!" I exclaimed, stamping my feet. "I am not some kind of genetic mutation. I'm just…different. I never asked for this!"

"You have Epilepsy; therefore, you are expendable."

I throw my hands up in the air in agitation and I look over at the door which I'd come through, then down at the Zen garden, filled with compartments of rocks and sand and plants which had never grown naturally, had never felt sunlight or rain. They are not real rocks or sand or plants, but blood and bone and remnants of humans left behind. Who made this miniature horror show? Who left this here to prolong my agony? Sighing, I sit on the ground, my body hunched over as I tap my fingers against my helmet. What am I waiting for?

Before The UNSC-5 had taken over, I'd lived an ordinary, somewhat dull, life, limiting my social interaction with others in case I had a seizure and embarrassed myself. I was terrified of my parents dying, as they would naturally do. I'd sit in my lounge room with the blanket around me and think of all the adventures I'd miss out on after I died, and how unfair that was. I had not been raised in a religious family, had not participated in the rituals of religion. However, sometimes, alone at night in my bed, I'd think about God, and I'd wonder if He was real and if He was, why he'd cursed me with seizures.

I'd been worried the evacuation would bring on a seizure, and I would be left behind. Mother had packed my medication, my scripts, and had reminded me to wear my medical bracelet. She had kissed my forehead, telling me everything would be alright. But I worried I'd collapse on the side of the street and people would walk over me, trample me to death, too scared, too panicked to realise I was underneath them. Who would stop to help someone while the reactor was dispersing unimaginable quantities of radioactive isotopes into the atmosphere? To stop and help was to forfeit your own life.

The seizure would start with a tingling in my hands, and it'd move down to my legs. My knees would jerk, and I would begin rubbing my hands over my arms, plunging my fingernails into my skin. Sometimes, I even drew blood. And it would feel as though I was looking through a glass, darkly. As though the world had erected a thin, opaque wall around me, sealing me inside a coffin-like structure. I would remain that way, seeing and hearing, but unable to coherently communicate.

A thunderous boom interrupts my thoughts. My brows shoot up, and I look around the room. It's just Chippy and me as it has always been. Then, the cacophonous sound of bending steel, a blast of drumfire bombarding the void. I jump as the floor begins to shake, as though some creature is pounding it with enormous fists from below.

I turn to Chippy, hands clenching the sides of the little kitchen bench. "What the hell is that?"

"Unsure. It seems to have come from outside the void."

"No shit, Sherlock."

"There's no need to be rude."

I twist my fingers together and stare at the robot. "Rude? You don't even know what *rude* means."

"On the contrary, I understand more than you think."

My brows furrow as I pause, glancing around the room, listening. "Shhh."

"There is nothing out there," the robot chirps. "Only radiation. Death. Especially death."

"Would you just shut up for a moment? Let me think!"

"I cannot do that. I am programmed to be your companion until you die. I must voice my opinions, tell you the truth. Right now, you need to calm down."

"Why?" I scoff. "Why bother? Why bother sending me here at all if I'm just going to die? Why bother giving me medication?"

Chippy's red lights flash quickly. I shield my eyes. "You are a project. I am programmed to monitor you. You are an undesirable. They want to know how long you can survive without medication. They want to induce seizures."

My stomach drops, and I feel a rush of bile claw its way up my throat.

"Are you fucking kidding me? Who would be so inhumane? So, I'm some sort of lab rat? Why?"

"I cannot answer that."

"Why not?" I exclaim.

"I am not programmed to."

I ball my hands into fists and stare at the door. The knocking continues.

"Someone knocked on the flippin' door, if you haven't noticed."

"You might have a seizure. I might not help you."

I raise a dubious brow. "You mean you might not be able to?"

"I might not help you."

Chippy is programmed to provide medical aid, but the robot does not understand the neurological issues of humans. He doesn't understand how helpless, how inhuman— how mechanical—Epilepsy makes someone feel. Perhaps that's why I feel a strange kinship with the drone. It, too, is a machine. It has faults of its own.

"I can form my own opinions."

"Will you just shut up? No, you can't."

"But that's where you're wrong."

The drone advances towards me, its little propeller spinning faster than I have ever seen it spin before. The front panel, what I'd come to think of as Chippy's face, abruptly blazes with red, blue, and yellow lights, whirling and flashing with such a penetrative force my head begins to spin. I press my hand to my temple, squint my eyes.

"What the hell are you doing?"

The drone begins humming, the sound akin to that of a bee. It pauses in front of me, its lights dimming. "You didn't think you were put here for no reason, did you? If you're so safe here, why did they request you keep your helmet on?"

I stumble backwards, hands shaking. "They're coming to collect me," I stammer. "They *are*."

"Your helmet is a long-term video-electroencephalography monitor. My chip was installed to ensure you do not take it off. Your neurological deficit is a liability. It would take too long for you to die outside. While others died quickly from the accident at the Halina Power Station, most were evacuated safely, and will die in old age, of the long-term impact of radiation exposure. But those like you, those who would be resettled, but did not really have a life worth living, were taken elsewhere. They sent *you* here to die."

The loud thud hammers on the door once more, this time more insistent. Whoever, or whatever, is on the other side has no intention of going away.

"What's on the other side of that door?" I whisper, my breath hard in my chest.

"Why don't you open it?"

"What?"

"Open it."

"Umm…I don't think I will."

"Do it."

"No!"

"Open it!"

"Why don't you?"

The drone turns to face me, its buttons flashing slowly. "I have no hands, if you haven't noticed."

"Why do you want me to open the door?" I ask suspiciously. "Isn't this my prison?"

"It is up to you."

I roll my eyes. "I wish I had a gun. Something for leverage. Anything."

"But guns are fired. What if no-one had knocked on the door?"

"What does that have to do with anything?"

The drone beeps. "Guns are fired."

"So?"

"It would be you and your gun, alone."

I shrug. "But you're here. You'll protect me."

"You said I can't formulate my own opinions. Why should I protect you?"

The door rattles as the knocking recommences. I cross the room and press the side of my helmet against it, trying to hear more clearly. The surface is flat and shiny, like the outside of a stainless-steel refrigerator. It has been many months since I've been outside the void. I'd almost forgotten the door, imagined it had no handle, no lock, no hinges, nothing to get a grip on. To reach the void, one has to navigate a system of underground tunnels, each with various checkpoints and key codes. I sigh. Where is my family? I wonder. Are they housed with the desirables? The one without defects? My little brother Cain—only five years old—was born with a heart defect, though it repaired itself over time. A selfish part of me wishes it hadn't.

"It'll be alright," you'd said, your chin on my head as I wrapped my arms around your waist and nuzzled into your chest. "Once we wade through all this bureaucracy, we'll be free to build a new home, together."

"You promise?" I'd whispered. "You promise we'll find each other?"

"I promise."

The knocking has stopped. I strain my neck as I press the side of my helmet against the door as hard as I can, struggling to discern the noise. It sounds like muffled voices spoken through an old candlestick telephone, voices auditory but incomprehensible. Almost like a whisper.

"Hello? Is anybody in there?"

The lights flicker off, on, and then off. I shiver, as the totality of darkness envelopes me, touching me with the unpleasant feeling, the lack of intimacy, I'd experienced as a child, frightened, cold, alone. I inhale a deep breath, outstretching my hands, shaking as my skin loses its natural ability to report to me the whereabouts and nature of my surroundings. The air itself is thick, cold, motionless. It slams into me with a force so strong it clenches my bones, holding me still. My hands shake as the familiar tingle works its way from my fingertips over my hands, around my wrists and up my arms, weaving around my elbows and shoulders, only resting as it coils its way around my neck.

"Help!"

Chippy's mechanical arm stretches out to grab my helmet, crushing it with its mechanical hands, ripping my flesh within its metal fingers. *But you said you had no hands!* I thought. *You lied.* Blood spurts through the cracks in my teeth like a fountain as my screams echo through the blood and glass in my mouth, and a rush of hot chemicals pour from Chippy and slam into my face, burning me with the savagery of a thousand fires.

"The defective has been eliminated," Chippy says. "I am ready to accept your other test subjects for experimentation."

"It's about time.," says an unfamiliar voice. "We can't have people like *her* using all our resources. We've got more undesirables in the van outside. Cancer. We'll give them a little longer than her and leave them a gun this time," the man said darkly. "The beauty in this place gives them hope. But gosh, I like taking that away from them. Let's see who snaps first."

I close my eyes, screaming as the gel-like chemicals begin to melt my skin, my eyes sliding from my face. Voices echo around me, though they seem far, far away.

"Attention! Attention resident. Due to high levels of neurological deficiency, the High Council has ordered your immediate execution. This is not a drill."

THE JACARANDA HOUSE

It occurred to Thomas, as he veered from the main road and drove slowly into the cul-de-sac, that he had made a big mistake. He'd bought the old house without inspecting it, planning to turn it into an investment property. But after months on the market, he began to realise that despite its luxurious size, nobody would be making an offer any time soon. Following a few disastrous weeks of stress-induced alcoholic binges, musings of childhood memories climbing the Jacaranda trees, of missed days at work, of cataloguing images of the house and its blueprints, he decided it was finally time to buy a plane ticket, fly interstate, and see the house once again for himself.

By the time he pulled up into the driveway, the moon hung smoky and yellow behind thin scudding clouds, offering no silvery light to lessen the oppressive darkness. In front of the house stood the two large jacaranda trees, gently bending in the spring air with the floppiness of boneless limbs. As a child, people had told him the beauty of the jacaranda trees protected the house, sheltering it from their constantly cyclone-swept town, yet he found that hard to believe. Trees had no hold over people, no matter how beautiful they were. A loud crack ricocheted around the cul-de-sac behind Thomas, like the spluttering of an old car. He looked up and stared at the shock of birds speckling the sky, wings flapping frantically.

Thomas got out of the car and stared up at the house. It had always stood in a composed way, as if it had chosen solitude for itself; its occupants were something it could forego. The old roof sloped in the middle; the screen door hung precariously from its remaining hinge; the grass twisted around the letterbox like sea snakes slithering through a creek. The windows of the old house were oversized and divided like the compound eyes of a fly. Thomas stretched his arms over his head and sighed. He rarely took time off for himself anymore. He hoped coming back to the house, coming back to the place he had grown up, would provide some comfort, despite its desolate exterior. Lately, he'd started taking risks, purchasing things on a whim—like the old house. Though only in his early thirties, he felt at least ten years older. And despite his professional success, he had never felt more alone. He spent his days wantonly, embracing his self-imposed solitude. If he could not pull himself out of it, he thought, he may as well go along with it and see where it led him. He glanced down at his watch. 7.00pm. He'd look around quickly and go; it was likely Mary would still be at the pub.

Thomas sighed. He had never liked the house. Neither had his siblings. As children, they'd all had nightmares about the house. His brother had complained about the cold daily, even in summer. His sister complained of neck pains. And Thomas woke up every morning with a sore throat, as if someone had choked the life out of him. At first, his parents didn't believe them. And yet over time they, too, started getting sick. Both his parents complained of intense, burning feelings shooting through their chests. Several doctors ruled out cardiovascular issues, and yet the pain remained.

The key took a little jiggling, but the front door swung opened easily enough. At once, a harsh, unpleasant odour hit Thomas with the force of a cricket bat. The pungent, damp, fruity stench filled his nostrils as he shuffled inside, his nose twitching at the mixture of sweet berries and lavender perfume old church women sold at the market. Coughing, he made his way inside and into the living area, leaving the door ajar to air the house out.

When inquiring about the property, the real estate agent informed Thomas that people didn't seem to stay in the house very long. The neighbours couldn't remember the last time anyone lived there for more than three months. As an adult,

Thomas had learned the man who built the house had polished the floors himself, the living room parquet a pet project of his. Thomas looked around, inspecting the personal touches. The walls stood firm, and the window frames were strong, despite the age of the house. Old cobwebs laced the ceiling, settling comfortably on unused furniture. The new owner had a certain style. Thomas imagined a flat screen TV would look out of place, ugly. The floor had once been lined with a thick slab of carpet, but half of it had uncurled at the edges, exposing large areas of rotting wooden floorboards.

To the left was a small sitting area, with his mother's old, abandoned piano sitting in the corner. She had said music in the house created a heart within a home. Thomas pushed the thought from his mind. He should have knocked down the house years ago. True, he'd spent the three years after his parents' deaths in a drunken stupor. Yet a part of him, a darker part of him, was happy they were gone. His mother, though possessing great beauty and musical skill, did nothing with her talent. She'd sit in the loungeroom and paint her nails all day, cornflower blue, like his eyes. His father, though a loyal worker, had no real ambition. After a few months of living in the house, they'd begun to argue; his father quit his job, his mother stopped giving music lessons. They argued about money, about Thomas; several times they'd brandished knives, threatening to slit their throats.

Thomas had been at school the day they killed themselves. They'd abandoned him, their suicide pact evidence they had never loved him at all. They'd stabbed themselves, or each other, multiple times. He hadn't attended their funeral. He and his siblings moved in with their aunt, uncle, and three cousins following the deaths. Thomas stared at the piano. He didn't like to admit it, but after his parents' deaths he became less of himself and more of a nebulous spectre. His own hands, once skilled at making music like his mother, became useless, as though all the bones from his fingers had been removed. His teeth, once rich and strong, began to rot. And his heart, once filled with the excitement of life, began to melt, becoming nothing but a diaphanous mass not strong enough to hold anything but bitterness and sorrow.

Thomas stepped around the carpet cautiously. He'd have to have it pulled up as soon as possible. He ventured down the hallway until he reached the kitchen. His stomach sank. The roof had slightly caved in on the right and was almost entirely covered in moss, peppered with cavernous holes that buckled under the weight of the rotting frame. Large cracks ran down the greying walls, shaped like lightning bolts, with chunks of lichen and slime growing around the edges. Frowning, he continued to his sister's room.

"What the…"

It seemed he'd left the house and ventured into a cave. Around him, the walls were made of rocks; the formations resembled meringues, dinosaur scales, velvet curtains, moss, broccoli, coral, bones, lace, icicles, mushrooms. Ripples of gold on high white expanses put him in mind of baroque cathedrals formed over millions of years, not by human hands but something spiritual, something holy. Body frozen, Thomas felt as though he was in the bowels of the Earth itself, like the chamber could be part of something organic, something alive. Slowly, Thomas outstretched a hand and ran his fingers over the rocky surface below the light switch. The surface was powdered with reddish-grey lichen, saplings sprouting from the socket.

"No way…"

Hanging from the ceiling were long liana vines, their ends splitting into five different branches, curled at the end, resembling fingers reaching to grab someone. The second finger was longer and curved, so it became a circle, with several wraps at the top. Thomas shuddered; it was clearly a hangman's noose. *What if I can't afford to knock down this house?* he thought. *What if no-one buys this house? What if the investment leaves me bankrupt?* Thomas shook his head, yet the dejected thoughts lingered. While he knew no-one in his family had tied the noose, and suspected vandals had come in while the house stood vacantly—or maybe it was the previous owners who had abandoned the house?— he couldn't shake the feeling of uneasiness. His stomach did backflips within his rattled body. *You can't sell this house.*

Withdrawing his hand, he rubbed his forehead, its nails digging lightly into the small creases. Stomach churning, he stepped backwards, stumbling back out into the hallway. To the right was a small alcove that led to the three bedrooms. The bottom step squeaked as Thomas applied pressure on the staircase with his foot; he let out a sigh of relief, surprised the old structure hadn't swallowed him up. He looked to the right. The door of the smallest bedroom, his sister's bedroom, slightly off colour from the rest of the house, loomed over him like a giant as he turned the brass handle. The door swung open with a creak. There was a flash of brown fur as several rats dived for cover. Thomas wrinkled his nose in disgust. He'd have to get pest control in as soon as possible.

The bedroom was empty, save for a few water-logged cardboard boxes and the stale straw-like odour of decomposing rats. Pinching his nose, Thomas glanced around; the room was larger than he'd remembered, though still retained the built-in wardrobe his father had installed. He could imagine the room stripped back and painted, with new carpets and furnishings, though he knew it would take a lot of time and money, more than he was willing to spend. It'd probably be best to demolish the house and start again, he thought. He could replace it with two smaller houses and make more money. Thomas dry-swallowed and pressed his fingers to his temple. *It was a mistake to come back here*, he thought. *Why return to a house you so despise? But why leave? Stay in the house. This is your house.*

Don't leave us.

Grimacing, Thomas ran a tired hand through his hair and returned to the hallway. He hadn't been sleeping well lately—his tiredness was getting to him. Passing one of the remaining bedrooms, he paused at the third door on the left. His sister had demanded she have this room, despite the fact it was bigger, and he was older. Eventually, he'd conceded; his father had let him build a sheet fort in the attic for extra space. He stared at the doorway. It was crooked; the door leaned slightly to the left; the longer he stared at it, the dizzier he became. The room seemed hollow without his sister's presence. She'd killed herself the day after her eighteenth birthday. No warning, no note. Just a broken neck and a small funeral.

Shaking his head, Thomas made his way to the curved staircase that led to the attic, taking the steps two at a time. As he reached the landing he paused, hand firm on his side. He'd become lazy of late; a sharp stitch dug into the right side of his waist.

The door was ajar. Peculiar sounds drifted out into the landing, almost as though within the room was a raging wind howling with the urgency of a hungry child. The escaping air was thick and slightly muggy. He outstretched his foot and nudged open the door. For a moment, Thomas thought he'd somehow returned to the dining room, for it seemed he had stepped into another cave. Except this time, the stalactites were made of ice. The left side of the wall was hard and high, akin to imposing cliffs sculpted from rock by briny waves. The rocky walls were creviced, patterned with geometric shadows an off-shade of white that could make blank pages seem grey. Flickers of azure specs painted the walls so small one might almost miss it.

The room was warm when his brother was alive. He'd killed himself on his fifteenth birthday, repeatedly stabbing his own neck with an ice-pick. Now it was cold, the frigid air holding him in place, keeping him in the room, wicking away his body heat until he felt completely frozen. Gulping a lungful of frozen air, Thomas pushed his way through the oppressive cold; his breaths were ragged coughs. Heart thudding, Thomas stumbled from the room, sprinting down the stairs as fast as he could without falling, bursting through the front door and into the garden. Dropping to his haunches, he closed his eyes, thumbing his temples, feeling sick to his stomach as the warmth of the sun flooded his body. He had to be ill. There was no other explanation. He had to be seriously ill. But what kind of illness would cause such an abstract visage, would cause him to succumb to such realistic hallucinations?

Thomas sat cross-legged on the driveway, staring up at the house. His heart thundered so heavily inside him he thought it would burst from his chest and land on the concrete beside him. Maybe he had fallen asleep? He pinched his arm. Nothing happened. He dug his nails into his hand. Still nothing. Thomas looked over his shoulder, at the other houses in the cul-de-sac. It seemed fitting they were positioned in a dead-end street, for they were lifeless and devoid of colour, clinging to their plot of land, stubbornly refusing to die. The great husks of derelict buildings seemed to belong together—the remnants of shattered glass in rotting wooden window frames, weed-infested gardens, and untiled roofs stood together, united in their abandoned despair. Thomas supposed people could have occupied the houses, yet he couldn't think of anyone who'd choose such unwelcoming dwellings to live in. He'd never understood why his mother refused to leave her family house. She'd been adamant about moving the family in after her parents had committed suicide. She wanted to preserve their memory, she'd said. But who in their right mind would move into such a depressing place? The only person who'd be willing to buy the house now would have to be a company with plans to demolish the entire cul-de-sac altogether. He imagined a neat row of houses with high-security gates and cameras. Maybe one of them would have a swimming pool?

Thomas gritted his teeth, pushing away his ambitious thoughts. There was no way an actual cave could exist inside the house. He *must* have been hallucinating. He'd been thinking of his parents of late, dead and buried for several years. Perhaps his thoughts of them conjured up a surreal manifestation? Pursing his lips, he plucked up the courage to pick himself up from the ground. He looked up at the Jacaranda trees. The slender, reddish-brown branches bent at odd angles, like broken, twisted limbs. The twigs, long, like outstretched fingers, were crooked, bending at odd zig-zagged angles. When he'd first arrived at the house the tree was in bloom, a spectacular lavender hue; now, the branches were empty. He'd get them cut down as soon as possible. Leaving them would blemish a new, neat neighbourhood.

Thomas tugged at his hair, stumbling backwards. Unease blossomed within him, yet he couldn't move, couldn't turn away from the house. His feet felt glued to the driveway. With each beat of his thudding heart, they grew more burdensome, as though they were set in the concrete. His mind urgently screamed at him, willing him to run, to get away from the house, but his body refused to move, as though it was stuck on a train track, waiting to be destroyed, waiting to become nothing more than fragments of blood and bone.

Panic seized him. He pressed his hand to his neck, coughing as his throat seemed to close, and his head filled with what felt like air. Without warning, his body moved of its own volition, each step dragging his body closer towards the house. The muscles in his legs burned as he told them to stop, to turn around, but they pushed on, pulling him closer to the front door. Pain sheeted through his body like a sharp-toothed creature devouring him from the inside. Eyes wide, he screamed incredulously as his body, as though pulled by invisible hands, was dragged up the driveway and towards the house. He dug his fingers into the bottom of the doorframe, screaming as his nails were pulled backwards, ripped off, exposing bloodied, pink skin. Clutching to dear life, he tried to hold on as hard as he could, clinging to the last vestiges of hope as his fingers broke, snapping backwards.

"No!" He cried, screaming. "Let me go! Someone! Help!"

He dug his broken, bloodied fingers into the carpet as hard as he could. He sunk his teeth into the carpet, kicking at the force that held him. Pain seared through him as his teeth separated from his gums, and he was dragged up the stairs and towards his old bedroom.

"Please! Stop! Anyone!"

The bedroom doorframe was warped, twisted, as though someone had moulded it from clay. It now appeared to be an immense gaping mouth, with shards of wood sticking out like two rows of pointed teeth. An assortment of prehensile vines, roots, and branches spat out from the room, twisting around Thomas's arms and legs like a vice, crushing his flesh and bones. A small segment of his ribcage broke from his chest, the snapping sound ringing in his eyes as loud as an emergency alarm. Blood spilt over his lips as Thomas struggled against the bondage. Screaming, he stared at the vine as it slowly grew visceral, the slender stem replacing plant with flesh, filling with bones; the leaves at the end of the stem elongated until they became slim, spindly fingers, with ten cornflower blue flowers sprouting at the end; the flesh of the vine twisted like gnarled branches, wrapping around his throat.

I don't want to do it, John. The light voice of his mother drifted in and out of the room. *But I can't do this anymore. The pain is too much...*

His father's voice whispered in his ear. *I can't do this either, Eleanor. This is too much to bear. The pills aren't working. Nothing is working.*

Around him, the darkness gathered like smoke, yet moonlight flickered through the window, the pool of yellow light speckling the room, like the flickering streetlamp outside. His family stood in the doorway. His parents' chests were bloodied, weeping from stab wounds. His sister's neck was bent at an impossible angle, her eyes wide and blank. Frozen blood congealed around a gaping hole in his brother's neck.

Don't leave us, his brother gasped, his voice throaty. *Stay.*

Thomas's head felt like it was exploding. Short, ragged breaths escaped his mouth. Lungs aching, he blinked as swirly specs of light danced before his eyes, then faded, as the room went black.

Stay with us forever...

TRANSPLANT

Lilith had the surgery on her eighteenth birthday. INTEGRATE was the leading research facility on heart failure. Using 3D bioprinting, they'd given her a new heart and a promised eight more years of life. The process had been easier than she'd expected. Her heart had been scanned with an MRI machine, creating a digital render of its shape and size. Her blood cells had been converted into stem cells, and then converted again into heart cells. The resulting hydrogel mixture became her bio-ink, to be used with a 3D printer. At first, Lilith had feared the process. Her specialist told her the bio-ink would be printed layer by layer onto a biodegradable scaffold, providing a structure on which new cells could grow, forming the exact shape of her heart. After a slice of birthday cake, she'd gone into surgery, and three days later her hearts cells joined and began to beat like a real heart. The following month, the scaffold was removed, and she'd had the life-saving transplant.

But now, eight years later, the ticking had begun.

Lilith sighed. She had lived in the small town all her life, trying her best to dodge the incessant busybodies and liars who inhabited the red brick houses all neatly lined up in a row. It wasn't that Lilith didn't want to leave—she just did not know how. Her loneliness hung around her like an old coat she could not shrug off. And while she was free to do what she wanted, she wasn't sure what that should be.

"Mum! Look at me, Mum!" Eleanor said. "Look at me now!"

Lilith turned the page of the book she'd been reading. She was not a particularly talented woman. She was not intrinsically artistic. Yet she longed for adventure outside her mundane life, the adventures other women had in books.

"See? Are you looking, mum? See?"

Lilith looked over the railing of the veranda. Her daughter swung from the lower branch of a tree. The girl was seven. Lilith did not know where the time had gone. One minute she was pregnant, the next minute her daughter rode her bike to school by herself.

"What am I supposed to be looking at?" Lilith asked. The girl was upside down. Her long plaits hung past her elbows. Her cheeks were ruddy. "You'll fall, you know."

"You're not looking!" Eleanor whined. "This is why you haven't got any friends, Mum. You don't listen!"

Lilith smiled. "People need other people to survive, but some people aren't wanted by others at all."

"What do you mean? Is that from one of your books?"

"I'm talking about having friends. Did you know a wolf has its own language?" Lilith asked. "We often think of the 'lone wolf' as a rugged individual, a mysterious man who doesn't need anybody else. But nobody really wants to live this way, and neither do wolves. Yes, I might not have any friends, but I have you. I am not alone." She placed the thin bookmark between two pages. "Wolves may go through periods alone, but they're not interested in lives of solitude. They need other wolves, and they are needed by other wolves in return. Maybe that's the difference between wolves and people."

"You never make any sense. And you're not looking!"

Lilith followed her daughter's gaze up into the thin branches of the trees. Two crows sat perched atop two mangos, their claws piercing the flesh.

"Did you know that birds are omens, or forecasters of events?" Lilith asked. "They are a link between the earth and the heavens, of transcendence and eternal life. They are messengers of the gods."

Her daughter raised a curious brow. "Really?"

"Yes. Birds are the disembodied human soul, free of its physical constrictions."

"You're not making sense again, Mum!"

Lilith smirked and returned her nose to her book. "You're a child. You don't make any sense, either."

Eleanor grumbled and climbed higher up the tree. Lilith didn't dislike trees; she had never shared the same joy of climbing them as her daughter. There were many joys she and her daughter did not share. Lilith liked to make cakes. Eleanor didn't eat them. Lilith liked to read books. Eleanor painted. Yet, they were similar in their indifference to each other's passions. They respected each other in a way only a mother and a daughter could.

"Look how high I am, Mum!" Eleanor called. "Look at me now!"

Lilith looked over the pages of her book. There had been a fire in the area, three months ago, yet the giant mango trees had been spared. She and Eleanor lived on the edge of the little town, on three acres on the side of the gully closest to the dam. Their house had been walled in by the burnt cypress trees, surrounded by the brittle plumes of dead branches, their crackling underfoot out of sync with the rhythm of her walking as Eleanor made her way inside the house each day after school. Yet the mango trees were defiant. Nothing, and nobody—no matter how violent or erratic—would tear them down.

Eleanor stood on the tallest branch, her little body swaying in the afternoon breeze, her thin arms clenching the trunk as tightly as she could. Lilith wondered what her daughter was thinking. In her own fantasies, she climbed the tree with her, and all her fears of motherhood dripped away. In her dreams, Lilith became part of the tree itself, watching as the crows gathered above her, their wings forming truncated crosses against a leaden sky in which storm clouds gathered, dark and ominous, promising a terrible and fierce fate. The ashen landscape grew larger around her as the trees became a forest, the shadows growing larger as the thin fingers of darkness stole the remnants of the day, so quickly darkening the sky Lilith thought she was slowly going blind. Lilith smiled. For a moment, Eleanor was part of everything around her: the dilapidated fences, the hollowed, lichen-covered orange trees, the wind passing through the house akin to a travelling god, airy and curvaceous, like the gossamer gown of the woman Eleanor would one day become.

"You look so small, Mum!" Eleanor called.

Eleanor was now but a spec of white overalls in the dense canopy above. Lilith wondered how she'd come to birth such a child. When Eleanor was born, she'd had nothing. Her dreams of a house and a family seemed vague and illusory. Her ex-husband drove the same old rundown car he always had, working the same job he would never leave. After their divorce, she'd sat in her old station wagon out the front of the supermarket in which he worked, watching him bag the same old groceries with the same old smile. Lilith liked Eleanor's father, but did not love him.

"Are you looking at me?"

Lilith nodded. Eleanor threw a mango down to her and it rolled over the broken leaves. Lilith slipped a piece of paper in her book and walked over to the tree. She picked up the mango and held it to her nose. It smelled rotten.

"Eat it, Mum!"

Lilith wrinkled her nose in disgust and threw the mango into the garden. "Come down, now, Eleanor. We'll go and get lunch."

"You're not looking at me, Mum! Can't you see?"

Lilith looked over to the tree and pressed her hand to her heart. *Tick tock, tick tock.* She pursed her lips, frowning. The ticking reverberated within her whole body, pushing against her temples until her head ached. A single tear ran down her cheek. How could she tell her daughter the heart transplant that had saved her life would one day kill her? That she had only been able afford to rent the heart, and that she'd have to give it back? INTEGRATE would be coming any day now to take it away, and she still hadn't saved up enough money to buy it.

"Hello?"

Lilith jumped. "Oh! You startled me."

A tall man walked over to the veranda. Lilith looked him up and down. He was unkempt, but not unclean. She was mistrusting by nature, yet he didn't seem like he'd steal from her, or harm her or Eleanor in any way. His skin was darkened by the sun, his fingers and teeth yellowed by cigarettes. But his smile was warm and welcoming, his skin soft as he shook her hand.

"I knocked a few times on the front door but no-one answered. The woman in the corner store said you had a room for rent. Is it available? It's just for the one night. I'm John."

"Lilith. It's thirty dollars for the night, fifty if you want to park your car in the backyard instead of on the street. You're welcome to share dinner and breakfast with us if you want. Oh, and there's an empty shelf in the fridge if you have your own food. You can have alcohol, but if you get too drunk, I'll have to ask you to leave. I have a young daughter."

She pointed up at Eleanor, still in the tree. The girl stared down at the man with an inquisitive expression on her young face. "Capiche?"

"Capiche."

Lilith smiled. "Do you have a bag or something?"

John shook his head. "I'm just passing through. I've got a razor, soap, toothpaste, and a toothbrush in my pocket. And my wallet. That's all I need for now."

"Okay. Well, you can use the towel that has 'guest' embroidered on it. It's on the rack in the bathroom."

"Thank you."

"Great. Oh, money up front."

John fished the thirty dollars from his pocket and handed it to Lilith. She crumpled it with her hand and shoved it in the pocket of her jeans. "Cool. Follow me."

She looked up at Eleanor, swinging from one of the branches of the tree. "Stay up there for a minute. I'm just showing the man to his room."

Eleanor nodded and climbed higher up the tree.

Lilith led him inside. Her grandparents had bought the house in the 1940s, after they were married. It had been in the family for three generations; her parents had left it to her in their will. Once, it had been grand, one of the first houses built in the area. But over the years it had fallen into dilapidated disrepair. Lilith had tried to make it as homely as she could with the little money she made from the bed-and-breakfast. It was hard work but rewarding.

Lilith directed John down the hallway to the guest room. It had been unused for some time, and the door creaked as it opened. She provided guests with blankets, a table by the window, a mirror, a small wardrobe to hang their clothes, and a large four-poster bed, the canopy made of soft black silk and white lace trimmings. The walls were painted a light lemon colour, and the cream carpet was thick and soft.

"I know it's plain, but some guests stay up to a month and put pictures on the walls." She pointed to the empty hooks on the wall. "It's pretty warm in here," Lilith said. "The bed is comfortable. You're welcome to make it your own."

"Thank you."

Lilith nodded. "My only rule is that I don't want you talking to my daughter. Got it?"

"Got it."

Lilith pursed her lips and returned to her seat outside. Eleanor sat on one of the higher branches, staring down at her.

"Why do people come to stay with us, Mummy?"

Lilith smirked. "So I'm not stuck talking to you all the time."

Eleanor frowned. "You're lying again. You're always lying."

Lilith thought of the unopened wine in the fridge. She usually drank when Eleanor went to bed, but today she was tired and didn't want her guest to think her an alcoholic. Even if she was one, she knew it was best not to let anyone else know. She looked up at Eleanor in the tree. The girl stared down at her.

"Are you ever going to come down from that tree?" Lilith asked.

Eleanor shook her head. "This is my home now. This is where I'll live forever. It's nicer up here, you know. Better than the smelly old house. Why can't we just move away?"

Lilith pursed her lips. "You know why."

Eleanor raised her brow and looked at her in such a way that she did not seem to be a child, but an adult. "You know he's not coming back, Mum. He's not going to walk through the door and ask for a room. Stop waiting for him. You and I are doing just fine, Mum. We don't need him. I'll be a teenager soon and I can get money for your heart operation, and we can live here without anyone needing to help us."

Lilith scoffed. "You're seven years old. Where you get these ridiculous ideas from, I will never know. Come on. Lunch."

"Can I eat it in the tree?"

"No. We'll eat with our guest. Now come on! I'm hungry."

They had hot chip sandwiches and lemonade for lunch. John heaped a pile of chips on his plate, but only ate a few before claiming he was full. Beads of sweat built up around his forehead. His eyes flickered to his mobile every few minutes, as though he was expecting an important call.

"What do you do for work?"

John looked up from his uneaten lunch. "Salesman. I sell ties."

Lilith raised her brows in disbelief. "I didn't know there was such a demand for ties."

"You'd be surprised."

"Can you be my mum's friend?" Eleanor piped. "She doesn't have any, you see."

"*Eleanor!*" The girl poked out her tongue. "Don't be so rude."

John smiled. "I'm sure she meant no harm. Tell me—is this your only source of income? I don't mean to pry; it's just my parents are thinking of starting a bed-and-breakfast. They have a few spare rooms now all their children are adults. I want to know if it's a viable business."

Lilith nodded. "This is it. I need to find extra work to pay for surgery, but there's nothing out there. Eleanor's dad sends money occasionally, which I'm thankful for, but I wish more people would come to stay."

"I'm sorry to hear that," John replied. "May I ask what surgery? You don't have to tell me. My mum always said I ask too many questions."

"Sounds like this one here," Lilith said, pointing at Eleanor. "I need a new heart. Mine is past its due date."

John nodded. "That's through INTEGRATE, right? My dad got a new kidney through them. Cost him an arm and a leg, but he managed to get a loan and pay it back."

Lilith sighed. "I wish it were that easy to get a loan. I spent so much money just to see the specialist to tell me what I already knew. Do they think money grows on trees?"

"Does money really grow on trees, Mum?" Eleanor piped.

Lilith smiled. "If you plant the right seeds, honey. But they're really hard to get."

John yawned. He stretched his arms over his head and flexed his fingers. "I might go for a siesta. I've been travelling all night and all morning."

"Selling those ties?"

"Yep. I'm on my way to a sales convention. Need to rest before I set off again."

"Okay. Well, let me know if you need extra blankets," Lilith said. "I'm happy to help you with anything you need."

"Good to know."

John waved and made his way into the guest room. Eleanor stuffed a handful of chips in her mouth, chewing noisily. Lilith rolled her eyes. She didn't know what she would do if she couldn't get a new heart. Who would care for Eleanor?

The afternoon passed slowly. At 6.00pm, Lilith made dinner and put Eleanor in the bath. She set the table and served John his meal.

"Spaghetti. My favourite."

Lilith smiled. "That's good. I was going to make garlic bread, but I forgot to buy the garlic from the store earlier."

"Ah. Won't you eat with me?"

"Oh, no. I'll eat later. Eleanor's the one with the appetite."

John grinned. "She seems like a great kid. I was wondering—and you don't have to answer—if your heart problem is genetic."

Lilith shrugged. "I'm not too sure. Eleanor rarely gets sick, but she has a check-up every three months just in case. So far, so good."

"That's good. But Eleanor's on your INTEGRATE health plan just in case, right?" John asked, twisting the spaghetti around his fork.

"Of course. I don't want to be unprepared if she encounters

problems in the future. I'm just worried about it, is all. It's so expensive. Plus, you need two signatories for the loan, and I have no idea where Eleanor's father is. I don't have any other family. I guess I'm hoping for the best. I don't want her to go through this. I've never been more stressed in my life."

John nodded, tipping salt onto his spaghetti. "What about this place? Couldn't you sell it?"

Lilith nodded. "I could, but then we'd have nothing. I can't lose this place. I put a lot of work, and a lot of money, into it. I'm not giving it up without a fight."

As the daylight faded, Lilith and Eleanor ate their meals, and John went for a shower. Lilith read Eleanor a story and put her to bed, then made her way outside and onto the veranda. The soft wind grew stronger, thick and crisp, its fingers stroking Lilith's skin with soft intimacy. She looked up. Heavy clouds blotted out the stars; the moon was a wraith-silver disc hanging low in the sky. The air thickened. Lilith rolled up her sleeves and wiped her hand across her forehead.

"Mind if I join you?"

John leaned against the doorframe, a glass of water in his hand. Lilith gestured to the wicker chair beside her and he sat down, placing the water on the little table between them.

"What are you going to do when your INTEGRATE health plan lapses?" John asked.

Lilith bit down on her bottom lip. "To be honest, my health plan *has* lapsed, and I don't have the money to pay for a new heart." She wrapped her arms around her waist. "I don't know how long I have. Plus, I need to make plans."

"For Eleanor?"

"Yeah. I mean, I *do* have a sister, Sally, but she lives a few hours away. I hardly see her. Eleanor will need to change schools. I haven't even written my will yet."

"You do understand the consequences if you can't afford a new heart, right?"

Lilith took a deep breath and pinched the bridge of her nose. All her money was in the house, and she wasn't sure if she could get a second mortgage. "Yeah, I do."

John stood up. "The ticking has begun, hasn't it?"

Lilith frowned. "How did you know?"

John walked over to the balcony and looked up at the sky. "You can feel it, can't you? The ticking? You must have known they'd send me."

Lilith's hands trembled at her sides. Her jaw dropped in a silent scream of horror. She could feel sweat drench her skin, the throbbing of her own eyes, the ringing panic vibrating in her ears, the thumping of her borrowed heart against her chest. Her muscles tightened, ready for action, yet she couldn't move. She couldn't even blink.

"I'm going to ask you to give me the child," John said.

"You said you sold ties! Please, just take me instead," she gasped. "I'll go with you! I'll go. I promise."

John pulled a pair of handcuffs from his pocket and slapped them against his palm.

"You have no credit. We'll be taking the house, but even that isn't enough. Now, we can do this the easy way or the hard way."

Lilith sprang to her feet, hands clenched. She thought of Eleanor, her little Eleanor, asleep in her bed. What would they do to her? She knew they wouldn't allow her to live with Sally, not when Lilith hadn't paid her debt. Lilith understood her body would fail her eventually, but to surrender herself now would be to give up her last chance of freedom.

"You can't run, Lilith." John's brows were furrowed, his forehead creased with heavy lines. His eyes were sunken and downcast. He looked tired. Lilith wondered if he liked his job, if he liked tearing families apart.

"Please," Lilith whispered. "Please don't do this. I'll give you everything I have." She dropped to her knees and pressed her palms together. "For the love of God, I'll give you everything I have. Just don't take Eleanor. I'm begging you."

John shook his head. "Tick tock, Lilith. Your time is up. You knew the rules. Everyone needs to abide by these rules so INTEGRATE can continue making organs. If we take away the profit motive by allowing people like you to default on organ loans, then we may as well stop producing organs altogether. It's that simple."

Lilith grabbed John's legs, clasping them tight. "You can't do this! Eleanor needs me!"

"And we need organs for sick children," John said, pushing her off him. "Eleanor is healthy."

Lilith's stomach dropped. Her mind flickered to the two crows perched within the mango trees earlier that day. She should have known this was coming. "What are you saying?"

"Give me the child."

"No!"

John reached into his pocket and pulled out a taser. It was small and black, with a yellow handle. "Did you know that each time the heart beats, it charges, and discharges, stored electricity? In between beats, the heart automatically goes into a brief recovery mode called diastole." John turned the taser over in his hand. "In that tiny window of recovery time, a sudden jolt of electricity could cause the heart muscle to go into ventricular fibrillation, which is essentially the first stage of a heart attack. The heart begins to pump erratically, if at all, and blood pressure drops to almost nothing, leaving no oxygen for the brain."

He aimed the taser down at Lilith. "If I shoot you with this, it'll definitely be painful. But imagine what it would do to a child."

"Don't you dare!"

John dropped to his haunches, his face inches from Lilith's. She could feel his hot breath against her face. "You're disposable. She's not."

"Please!"

The taser tensed every muscle in her body, rendering Lilith unable to move. Her body rolled onto its side with a soft thud. The pain was akin to what she imagined it would feel like to be struck by lightning. She could not move. She could not speak.

"We can't make exceptions, Lilith," John said.

Lilith gasped. "You…you have to let me go. Eleanor needs me. Do you even have a heart?"

John grinned. "Was that supposed to be a joke?"

Tears streamed down Lilith's face. "Does human life, human

suffering, mean nothing to do?"

John gently stroked her hair, pushing it out of her face. "I should be asking you the same question. Imagine how scared your little girl will be when she's strapped to the operating table, anaesthesia slowly sending her to sleep before the surgeon cuts out her heart. Do you think she will cry for you? *'Mummy,'"* he mocked. *"'Why would you do this to me, Mummy? Don't you want me? Don't you need me? Don't you love me? Did you ever love me?'"*

"You bastard!"

"Mummy?" Eleanor stood on the veranda, tiny hand clasping the stuffed rabbit Lilith had bought her for her birthday. She rubbed her eyes and stifled a yawn. "Mummy, what are you doing?"

"Run!" Lilith gasped. "This man…he's a…bad omen. The crows…" She thought of their earlier conversation. Her broken heart pounded as she thought of a life without her little girl. "They were sending us a message, love! You have to run!"

Eleanor's little face twisted in confusion. "Now? Where are we going?"

"Just go!"

"Is this pretend?"

Lilith shook her head. "I'm not lying this time. I'm not pretending. Please! Go!"

John slammed his boot down on Lilith's face. Her nose shattered instantly, the audible crunch ringing through her ears with the intensity of an alarm. The blood was hot as it pooled out of her nose, running over her top lip and into her mouth. Lilith watched in frozen horror as John scooped up Eleanor under his arm and carried her around the side of the house, her little body squirming in his strong grasp. Lilith pushed herself to her feet and stumbled after them, her heart pounding as furiously as it ever had, her arms outstretched, reaching for her precious Eleanor.

"Give her back! Eleanor! I'll give you everything! Give her back!"

John pushed Eleanor into the back of the van. A tall blonde woman reached out and strapped her to a chair, pulling a hood over the little girl's face. She shut the door.

"No!" Lilith wailed. "Give her back!"

John stopped at the passenger door and turned to face Lilith. His face was stony, mouth set in a straight, grim line.

"Tick tock, Lilith. Tick tock."

He climbed into the car and shut the door. Eleanor leapt towards the door, tugging on the handle. It wouldn't open. She reached through the window. She tugged on the inside handle. John twisted her wrist. He pushed her away. She fell to the ground, her head slamming into the side of the curb. Her chest flooded with indescribable pain that had nothing to do with her transplant. She'd lived with a broken heart for years, but she knew her heart had broken in a way INTEGRATE could never fix.

I might not have any friends, but I have you. I am not alone.

THE EAGLE

I didn't know her by name, or what she truly looked like. But I would watch her like a hawk, my wings like the arms of puppets jerking pointlessly through the lazy air. I knew this land, knew the depth of it and felt no fear as I crisscrossed and swooped like the dirt of a mustering storm, always spinning, spinning, spinning. Ever since the transformation, I found it hard to stay still for long periods of time. But she would often make me pause.

I long suspected her of witchcraft. Over the course of the months I spent with her, I realised the most terrifying creature in her gully, was she. I learned her powers were not immoral, but scientific—she was able to manipulate the land around her, stretch it, bend it, entwine it within her fingers, tell night to pass, and day to come forward. That was when I knew her to be part of everything around her, the dilapidated fences, the hollowed lichen-covered orange trees, the wind which passed through the house like a travelling god, airy and curvaceous, like the gossamer gown of a woman rippling in her wake. Now, the air around me is still, and as I curl my talons around the edge of the water tank, I feel both place and time to have changed. I feel her once again, prodding me to look deeper into the tank, to recognise the scent of her bones and the discarded remains of her body curled up and alone.

To get to her house, I had to traverse a white landscape of edgy, pointed plains, which I saw as an endless stretch of colourless nothing—a void of which I had now lost all interest to see. I remember the cleanness of its horizon lines, its rocky, shifting craters; now, twenty years later, the image manifested itself in my eagle mind, perfectly rendered, as though not a day had gone by.

Of course, there were certain times when the openness of her lands, the height of the mountainous ranges enclosing her little house, made navigation hard for me. I struggled to remember the intimate creases of the grasses, the exact sound of the rain falling upon the leaves of the forest in the gully, but I fought with all I had to maintain the intimacy of the landscape I once took for granted. I struggled with the memory of uprooted trees after a wild storm, the creek bed which had since been dammed to create a little ornamental lake, more for looking at than for partaking in its natural resources.

The place for sitting is not inside her house but on a handcrafted bench located under an olive tree. As I dive towards her house, broken wing lagging me, pausing at the halfway point between the gully rim and the old, overturned rowboat half buried in the grass, I sense the bench has been unattended for some time. I wonder if she sat in this very spot overlooking the terrain, and I wonder what she felt seeing her house look so small in the distance. I perch myself on the bench. When I had my arm, I would gather firewood for her, tramping into the bush and over to the dam to check its level and the condition of the pump. I would climb the ladder to peer into the water tank, balancing my torso precariously on the edge. Afterwards, I would check the gas cylinder, disconnecting it if it was empty, replacing it with a full one. Sometimes, I would gather old newspapers and build a fire outdoors, and I would add to the firewood to help with the kindling of her indoor fireplace. While she never invited me in, I enjoyed performing these simple tasks for her, happy to find comfort outside a village that had shunned me. Sometimes, I would even clean her lavatory, my arm aching, cleaning the piss and shit the weary travellers left behind, and then contentedly weeding the garden to settle my stomach.

She had died in bird form. I could smell the blood on her short, hooked beak. I could smell the mud on her curved talons. I imagined her eyes as slabs of black marble, though unfocused, uneasy. I could smell the dirt on her long, jagged tail. When she had first taken my eyesight, I had imagined myself as a bird, weightless, free of the constriction of gravity. I imagined not being able to feel anything except the wind gushing through my wings as I sped through the air.

I remember shooting her down with the rifle, excited I had managed to load and shoot it with one arm, angry she had chosen to deny my sight from me, and the ability to become what she was: a master of herself. I knew she would never leave this place, and her bird body would rot. While one part of me wishes to know who she was as a human, another is content to have known her as a bird, in the form she had embraced. Tears run down my feathered face as I realise she had been forced to transform by the gigantic, feathered, long-limbed human, its razor-sharp teeth covered in blood. A part of me wonders if the creature had been trapped in limbo, stuck between human and animal, never accepting its form as its true nature. I wonder if it would come back, and whether that was why she had rebuilt the gate, had kept it closed, and remained vigilant.

I often wonder what she looked like, whether she was beautiful, or ugly. Whether she was white, or black. A part of me suspects the latter, for why else would she wear such a dark, thick veil to hide her features? Sometimes I wondered if she, too, had been sent to work for the rich white families in plantation houses, and had escaped her master, retreating into the gully to be alone without chains. Years ago, a little while after we had first met, and I still had sight, I knocked on her wooden door with a loud rap, startling her from her sleep. She'd opened the door slowly, as though fearing an intruder, and tilted her head ever so slightly to the left after realising it was me.

"You forgot to show me how to use the pump. And I don't know how to build a gate. Is there any point in fencing your house from the rest of the wilderness?"

"You know," she said in her quiet, gravelly voice, "I once saw a creature leap six feet in the air and over one of my fences. I was busy making a list of things to do when suddenly two wealthy white folks came into the gully in a great, rustling wagon. I told the townsfolk to stay away, but they drove the wagon at least three hours into the valley expecting to find a hearty fire with a veranda and a fortune teller to tell them their futures. But they never made it. The creature leapt out of the dark and plucked both man and son from the wagon. It pecked out their eyes and dropped their bodies on my doorstep. It was a gigantic creature, feathered, yet long-limbed, like a human. Its teeth were razor-sharp and covered in blood. So, there is no real reason to rebuild the gate, but I like to think by shutting a gate, by closing something, I am reminding myself to be vigilant at all times."

Be vigilant at all times.

Cautiously, I flap my single wing over to the windowsill and peer into the house. It had been a long time since my last visit to the gully. Everything feels so small. I remember visiting her and feeling as though the house was bigger than it was, suggesting she keep a gun in her room in case stray travellers dared to ransack her house, or burn it down altogether.

"I can't keep a gun," she'd said. "Guns are fired. There will be no fire in my gully."

"It's not a literal fire," I'd said. "You're an old woman living alone in a house in the wilderness. You take in strangers and feed them and clothe them and allow them to work for their lodgings. I could have killed you if I'd wanted to, the first night I came to you. You could be shot for saying the wrong salutation to those aristocrats."

"You don't have the capacity to kill. I know that."

"Because I have one arm?" I asked sardonically.

"No. Because us folk are thicker skinned. We weren't even born in the right skin, so we have to make do with what we've got."

The remark had fallen on deaf ears. Over time, I became accustomed to the two of us living together in unison. I kept an axe beside the bed and served soup as she told me of all the beautiful places she had visited throughout the world. She was knowledgeable about many things and wiser than anyone I had ever known. She told me about the martial eagles' eyrie, that had been part of the land for over fifty years. She told me about the eagle, how it liked to watch the koalas sashay backwards down the sapling trees, scramble on the ground on all fours, and tumble into the forest. She told me the scraggly cypress trees were her favourite, though she was worried about the soil erosion nearby, and what might happen in five, ten, fifteen, twenty years' time. She talked as though she would never leave this place, and I was inclined to believe her.

"The eagle's eyrie is a fork of a tall tree growing deeper in the forest," she'd said. "You can just see it if you squint your eyes and observe. Sometimes things simply appear to you if you let them. "

I'd squinted my eyes, but all I could see were trees in front of me, trees around me, and even more trees in the distance.

"You'll see it, in time," she'd said.

Now I wonder if the eagle was her former companion. She'd kept his teeth in a jar, his human teeth, proof he was no longer a bird. Now and then she'd take them out and press a single tooth to her lips. "You saved me," she'd say, pressing her weak hand against her stomach. "You saved me."

I wish I could remember things more clearly. My interest in the woman had been shallow, as my eagerness to learn had taken over. Finally, after so many years, I had been welcomed, instead of ignored. She allowed me to sleep and to rise when I wanted. She didn't ask me to cook her meals, or clean for her. Over time, I wanted to be like her. I wanted to know her magic, her secrets. I so desperately wanted to learn if there was any way to grow an arm, yet she told me to be patient, and I grew angry. I wanted to possess everything she possessed. I was disappointed in myself. I step backwards from the window and trip on a tree stump, falling on the cold grass. Although it is mid-morning, I feel the sun dropping behind the ridge, and I know the shadow of the light wobbles like waves in a sea. I feel nervous, startled. I feel like someone may be watching me. Glancing around, I see nobody, but I can hear the thunderous tune of my heartbeat, the tempo loosening as I realise I am alone in the gully. And still, I feel the need to be comforted. I have a sudden urge to tramp down to the bottom of the dam, up the slope of the forest ridge, and fly away on the wind right out of the gully. I want to escape the unused firewood, the dark, crumbly, rotten sticks; I want to kick the decaying boughs away from the house as if the wood was rotten at its very core. But I stand still, ears prickling as I hear the wilderness around me come to life, footsteps scurrying across fallen branches, flat leaves. I clench my fists, ears straining to determine who, or what, I know to be there.

"Show yourself!"

I perch on the ground, feeling unimaginably small, wishing I still had my hand to hold a whittling stick. I am no longer afraid yet feel as though I am waiting for something. Slowly, I breathe in and out, watching, waiting, for something so dark and unimaginable to announce itself. My stomach twists itself into knots, and suddenly, without warning, my bladder gives way and I feel hot urine run down my stick-thin legs, its heat quickly dispersing into the cold. This warmth is my making, I think to myself. I patiently wait for the absence of urine to unpick all the knots in me, but the feeling of wariness and trepidation does not abate.

"Hello?"

I flutter over to the water tank, rushing to spring up the wooden ladder. My single wing spreads to a triangular shape as I press my talons firmly upon the ladder rungs. Once, I had considered the spur-like protrusions a curse, but now I see their dexterity, their usefulness, in climbing the ladder of the tank. I stand there, clinging to the trim, my voice booming across the forest.

"Show yourself! Where are you? Coward!"

I forget the stiffness of my body, concentrating on holding onto the ladder. I remember how the house once looked, though now the blind landscape seems alien to me. I remember dreaming of visiting distant places, wandering from place to place, uncaring of how the world changed without me. I remember feeling isolated, and alone. And yet the seven months I had spent blind had opened my eyes to the reason I had visited the woman in the first place. I'd felt lost. I felt alone. Discouraged by life, ostracised by my village for being inadequate—*Who would marry a black girl with one arm? You're worth nothing. You can't sew, you can't dance, you can't cradle a child to your chest* — I had begun to eat my own heart, piece by piece, until I had nothing more to give. I had become undeserving of my human body. Carefully, I ascend the ladder, and for a moment, I imagine feeling cocooned by my ribcage, constrained within my flesh. As I reach the top of the ladder, I lean into the water tank. I remember the day the woman died.

I flutter down into the water tank, landing on her bloated body. I didn't want to lose her. I didn't want to embarrass her in front of the forest. I had shuddered as the bullet connected with her forehead, frightened when it bounced off her skin, and my feet slipped in my sodden sandals. There is no ugliness in this forest but believe me when I say I am ugly *within* the forest. Others do not seem perturbed by the death of the witch, the increased desolation of the sacred house. They go upon their business, warning children to stay away as the town grows around us, modernising and reinventing itself. A clear, cool day might have sapped this sadness from me, but there will always be an ugly forest growing inside my bird head. As the seasons change, and the colours seem to be all wrong, I realise time is a labyrinth.

A rustle of leaves in the distance disturbs my thoughts, and I turn to see a thin man scrambling through the trees, face pale, eyes clouded. He looks tired, and wanders into the gully, collapsing on the bench under the olive tree. I fly over to him, and he shields his face, as though frightened my talons will tear it to shreds.

"Please, don't hurt me! I'm tired; I just want a place to stay for the night."

"I don't keep a gun," I say. "Guns are fired. There will be no fire in my gully."

Suddenly, the man's tired and bloodshot eyes appear focussed. With as little warning as a lightning flash, he reaches up and slowly pulls at the skin of his face, scratching at it with the enthusiasm of a ballet dancer pushing through the pain of transforming her body into a structure it was never supposed to be. Blood and tissue fall away from him like string cheese, and I can see in his eyes the adrenalin as his body warms to a dark pink, and the bones in his back begin to unfold like cutlery in a rolled-up velvet pouch. Bone by bone, his skin elasticises as his shoulder blades expand, muscles stretching out, out, out, until they seem over seven metres long, and a single thought enters my mind, hard and sharp: this is a forsaken visage to behold. Two skeletal structures stretch out from his shoulders, creating three separate humerus bones sprouting from his bloodied scapula. Slowly, his fingers elongate, breaking, twisting, curving as they become talons, and the forest fills with a cold, yet pungent, sickly-sweet aroma, almost like the stench of a decomposing corpse. Blood and skin and muscle drape from his body, sagging like the breasts of an old, worn out woman. His body continues to transform, as feathers burrow out of his skin like parasitic mites. Gasping, I trip over my feet, and he takes one shaking step forward, wings outstretched. Droplets of blood fall from his battered bones, dripping on my face.

"Do not be afraid. She sent me."

"Will you teach me? She said you would be waiting for me."

"Have you seen her?"

"No. The witch took my eyes the moment I stepped into the house and told me to come back when I could see. She told me I would see a blind bird and I would learn once her eyesight returned. I can see you're no longer blind, yet you have only one wing. I have been living in this gully for many years," he added.

"You're the martial eagle," I murmur curiously. "She has your teeth."

"Yes. You're the white-tailed eagle."

I stare at his toothless mouth, permanently downcast, his gums a red bed of mountains lodged inside his jaw. His jaw itself is rotten, mouth dry, as though it suffered the propensity to crave high-calorie carbonated water, teeth grinding and clenching like it spent periods of neglected oral hygiene.

"Have you come for them?"

He nods. "I cannot eat. What did you do for her to remove your curse of blindness? Did you exchange your eyesight for a wing?"

"No!"

"You don't have to get angry. I am starved. Every morsel of food I consume tastes like ash. I have heard of another who had her hearing taken from her. The woman sought shelter from a storm, and the witch took her under her wing. She lived with the witch for three months, and then the witch cast her out, stealing her ears."

I flutter my wings impatiently, thoughts whirring. The witch is part of this gully. She is the eyes and ears of this place. She sees all, and she knows all. She is one with the gully, and the gully is one with her.

"Do you want to go inside the house?"

He nods.

Although it is only mid-afternoon, the sun sits low in the sky, a pale orange, casting shadows over the mountain ridges in the distance. I glance over at the olive tree I remember as a sapling, its thick trunk curving slightly in a peaceful way, as though the wind had gently nudged it and it had moved of its own accord. I didn't plant the olive tree, and neither did the witch; she had told me it was here when she arrived, almost smothered by thick foliage, frozen still in winter. While I do not wish to leave her body alone in the water tank, we go inside the house. I am uncertain of how I should move my limbs. As a human, I had walked contemptuously, almost with arrogant pride, as though I had to make myself better than others because they were born with two arms and white skin, and I was cursed with one arm and black skin. Now, I feel confined, as if houses are not for creatures such as myself. We go into the kitchen, and I reach out for the kettle, ears prickling as a strange gargling sound erupts from the back room. A heavy scent of eucalyptus floats under my nose, and I stare at the eagle man, yet he makes no response.

The room feels small, abandoned, as though all memories of my time spent here had evaporated. The eagle man fills a lamp with kerosene, and for a moment I am jealous he has retained a semblance of fingers. His wings are ugly, deformed. I wonder if the witch designed him that way on purpose. He is colourless and indistinguishable.

"I don't know what I'm doing in here," I whisper, shocked at my admittance.

"I do," he replies firmly.

The stove is cold, but the two of us manage to light a fire, the heat growing quickly within the room. I heat the remains of vegetables and turn them into soup, and we hungrily slurp it with our beaks, hurriedly, messily, as creatures who have not yet mastered the eating habits of their species. The eagle man licks the saucepan, and I watch as he unashamedly flickers his tongue like a serpent, devouring every morsel of the soup.

Outside, a gunshot fires in the distance, and the eagle man drops the saucepan, mouth ajar as he glances at me with fear. My wing flutters in agitation, and I grasp a fire poker with my talon, chest heaving. I wonder why I am so afraid, and why I fear, shameful of being afraid. I wonder why fear and shame are synonymous.

The second shot comes almost as a relief—it allows me to let out the intake of air, but also form conclusions in my addled mind. Someone else is in the gully, someone who knows of the witch, and what she has done. The eagle man and I share a curious glance, and I wonder if he is thinking what I'm thinking. Someone else has come to reclaim their body.

I wonder if the owner of the gun has been transformed, but instead of descending into madness after a few years, has slowly accepted their fate as the creature they had become, living in a mad frenzy of confusion and denial, finally returning to the witch's house to enact their revenge.

"We should leave," the eagle man murmurs.

"No," I reply sternly. "We should stay. You need your teeth. "

"I also need my life."

Suddenly, an obtrusive thought pierces my mind. "I did not rebuild the gate."

"What?"

"I did not rebuild the gate," I repeat, heart thudding erratically in my feathered chest. "The witch always rebuilt the gate, kept it closed, and remained vigilant at all times. I have not been vigilant. I have been careless. A closed gate offers no invitation, but an open gate wields no weapons…We are trapped." I glance at the eagle man, frightened, my very bones shaking in my skin. "Describe to me how you look. Beforehand. I never knew what she looked like, and I have always been ashamed of being too scared to ask. The bullet hit her too fast, right through the head. There was no time to say goodbye. Please," I urge, surprised my voice is verging on the edge of hysteria. "Tell me what you look like, so I know which body is yours. Perhaps, we can find it."

The eagle man cocks his head inquisitively. "She kept it? After all this time?"

"*I* kept them. All of them. I was going to burn mine, but…it seemed a worthless waste of kindling. But I have not been down there, for the thought of seeing my body and being trapped in this hideous form fills my stomach with fear."

"Show me."

The door to the cellar is at the back of the house, down the thin hallway. We walk into the darkness, careful not to slip as we descend the rickety ladder. The eagle man gasps as we reach the earthy floor.

The cellar contains a small forest deep beneath the house. Within it is every plant and tree I had ever known to grow. Twisted vines, knotted branches, musty leaves left to rot on the earthen floor. And skin. Piles and piles of skin. Human skin stretched around the boughs and branches of trees, wrapped around vines and left to hang in the damp air. A slight breeze blows through the branches, and they rustle ever so delicately, as though keening to hear sounds within the wind. The stillness, the softness, is mesmerising, and yet a deep sadness hangs upon the air, like a weighty blanket drenched in water, covering the trees with a musty stench of decay. I feel generations of spirits around me, airborne whispers, bits of bark, the remains of the long-forgotten and deceased wrapping themselves around me. Years of cries and screams clasp my ankles so desperately I feel disinclined to take a step backwards, yet I am terrified to step forward. I feel the slow drag of the witch's magic entwine within my muscles, my flesh, curl around my torso, and shoot through my fingers, coursing through my veins. I gasp, breathing through

73

every pore, every feather of my body trembling as I feel the power swirl within me, my blood skittering through my bones.

Above, the shooting continues sporadically, as though the owner of the gun is firing shots purely for the sake of exacting terror. I don't know how long we wait, frozen in fear and anticipation, unsure of what to fear, or what to anticipate, petrified of the sight before us, of the dark magic weaving its wave through our bodies.

I turn to the man, body anxious. "You have learned to assume the form of an eagle, even though you are a man. Can you teach me how to adopt the form of a white woman, even though I am a bird? Can you give me one of these arms and attach it to my shoulder so I am whole?"

The eagle man stares at me with such inquisitive eyes I think he might laugh. Instead, he smiles sadly and places a heavy hand on my wing.

"You are mistaken," he replies gently. "I am an eagle who has assumed the form of a man. Look around you, at these trees, at this underground forest. What do you see?"

I frown. "I see trees, the same as you see."

"Ah. But I do not see trees. I see people."

"People?"

The eagle-man smiles sadly. "There are some enchantments that would take the form of one creature and transform it, transmute it until it is not what it once was. What looks like a tree is a person, what looks like a person is a tree. Every branch is an arm, every vine a wisp of hair. Do you understand what the witch has done? You are not her only transformation. This entire forest, this gully, is alive. But you killed her, and now we can never be released."

I glance at the scene before me, mesmerised by the horror. It is disgusting, yet beautiful. Still, confusion wracks my brain, and I am unable to grasp the jagged thoughts running through my mind. *Is every branch an arm? Is the forest, the gully, alive? Does that mean...*

"I am not like other men, and you are not like other eagles," he says. "I am trapped within this misunderstanding of who I am, and who I ought to be. I do not want to be this way — not understanding the ways of humans, their thoughts, their nuances, their passions. What do I need with passions? What do I need of love?"

He steps towards me, and I step backwards.

"I am not sure..." I whisper breathlessly, stomach knotting as I gaze at the trees around me. "I am not sure what you are telling me...but I think...I just wanted to be accepted..."

Gasping, I bite down on my tongue, startled by the sudden movement of the long creepers, twisted vines, and lianas slithering along the earth towards me. Vines dangle from the tangled canopy above, reaching like outstretched limbs, long branches snatching at my shirt. The long lianas, once attached to the countless hosts of skin-trees, climb towards the canopy and, clasping tendrils from stems, plunge thorns and spikes through my legs. Small shrubs spring to life as human hands uproot them, pushing them aside to shoot out and tug at my dewclaws, tripping so I fall backwards onto the floor with a thud. Screaming, I gasp as vines twist around my broad wing, knotting around my talons, digging into my flesh, piercing my bones, wrapping themselves around my organs.

"Please..." I gasp, struggling to breathe. "I just want my body back. I don't even want a second arm anymore! I don't care that I have dark skin! That is all...all I ever wanted. I remained here, waiting...but it doesn't matter...please..."

The eagle-man shakes with fury, eyes tearing in horror. "*That is all we ever wanted!*" he shouts, spittle running down his mouth. "*I just wanted my body back! I cannot stand to be what I am not!*" he screams. "*I am no longer whole, and you took that away from me. You killed the witch. I was her servant, yes!*" he bellows. "*But with her, there was still a chance! You took that away from me, from all of us! I cannot bear to be this hybrid human any longer! All I want is the sweet release of death, but I deserve to die an eagle, just as I was made. I deserve it...*" the eagle-man splutters, tears and mucus intertwining. His voice drops to a half-hearted whisper. "I deserve it, you fool. Who cares if you weren't born with the skin colour society thinks you should have? Who cares if you were born with one arm? You should have accepted yourself as you were. But now, because of you, we can never be free."

I stare at the eagle man in astonishment, guilt shaking me to my very core. I feel responsible for this creature, responsible for the motley assortment of skin and bones and vines and leaves squeezing the life out of me. While I know I am not like the witch, I know I am greedy and self-absorbed. I understand it was no trouble for the eagle man to ensnare me, for I had allowed it in my self-depreciating way. I had given up on myself, had allowed myself to think I was somehow incomplete as a black woman with only one arm, and in doing so, I had given up on him, and on all the others in this twisted menagerie of broken bones and fetid flesh.

"I no longer understand how it feels to fly," the eagle-man shouts, eyes bulging in pure anger and desperation. "My talons are useless! My eyrie is abandoned! I am no apex predator, no kleptoparasite. I do not understand how to be this hideous beast! I circle this dense, knotty environment, searching for a purpose, but I find nothing but this wretched house, this miserable place. It is ugly. *I* am ugly!"

I think of the gully, of its wild beauty. It was just as I had left it. There is no ugliness in the gully, at least, not to the untrained eye. The landform is luscious and green, water sloping between the cracks, eroding sharply into the soil. I wondered who or what created the gully, whether it occurred through vegetation clearing, deforestation, or dislodged soil from heavy rain. I wonder if a farmer once lived in the witch's house, or if she once farmed herself. Did she clog the downstream water bodies to form the gully herself? Was the gully once a barren landscape? Did she restore the landscape with her magic? Or perhaps she became the gully herself, surfeited of townships, eager to gorge herself on the spurs and hills around her. Why did I take this away from her, this majestic landscape, coloured in greens and reds and blues and purples, filled with the screeching cries of the humans trapped in animal form? I wonder if I have any right at all to have taken it from her. Did anyone have the right to take a life? Did I have the right to separate her from this place, her home?

The vines knot securely around my neck, and I gulp in a final breath, eagle tongue flopping out of my mouth, the remnants of fish bones and flesh still embedded within the longitudinal ridges. As the vines squeeze my carotid artery, I feel the blood on the sides of my neck slow, my heartbeat fall out of rhythm, my brain sending shockwaves through my body. I hear the shooting above, but it seems foreign, far away. Suddenly, I am struck with a sudden childhood memory of when I my parents would take me to see the travelling fair, and I would clench my fist over the middle of the balloon, pumping my fingers to alternate air from one section of the balloon to another.

The eagle man laughs as urine streams down my leg, and the sharpened vines, entangled with rotten flesh and broken pieces of bone, shoot through the air to impale my wing and my body. He lunges at me, claws shooting through my flesh, tearing at it, pulling it apart, frenziedly stabbing at my withered body, at the bloodied coils of my abdomen, blood circulating so quickly I vomit over myself. The eagle man smiles slyly, his guile rendering me irrevocably helpless, and I struggle to remain conscious.

"You see?" he thunders. "You see what you make me do to you? "

He leans over me, tongue outstretched, and licks the vomit from my body, hungrily smacking his lips.

"This is all your doing!" he shouts, hot, angry spittle flecking my face. "If I cannot be my true self, then neither can you! Oh, look at your tears," he mocks, licking them from my face. "You want me to believe you feel sorrow? You feel pain? You do not know the meaning of pain. I can see it in your eyes," he says. He stabs a sharp talon into the bed of my mouth and pulls out four of my teeth at once, and I open my mouth to scream, but no words escape.

"What did you do for her to remove your curse of blindness?" he demands, stabbing his claw through my bird-jaw. "What did you do?"

Blood gurgles in my throat, and I gasp, struggling to answer.

"Nothing..." I splutter, body shaking. "These are not my eyes. I stole them. I couldn't do it any longer. I couldn't live in a world of darkness. I stole them. I prayed and prayed, but nothing I did would return my sight, so I stole them. You don't know what it's like," I gasp, "to have no arm and no eyes. The world was already dark... Imagine how dark it became without my sight! I just wanted the light...I wanted to be light..."

The eagle man scoffs, stepping backwards. He stares at me, shooting a look of pure loathing and revulsion.

"Stole them off who? Who did you rob of their eyesight?"

Straining from the vines, I hesitate to answer. And then, as though sensing my distress and unease, the vines tug tighter around my neck, and the eagle man becomes nothing but a blur of colours swirling around me.

"You will not tell me? Ah, but you are a fool," he says, laughing. His laughter is not humorous but dark, threatening, like the crackle of thunder before an impending storm.

"You are but the mere mask of a woman," he says, leaning towards me intimately. "I have travelled the world, traversing with theatre troupes, actors, singers, playwrights. I know the masks of foxes, of bears, of parrots, of lions. I know the masks of false idols and false women. I have seen masks of wood, papier-mâché, grass, wood, cloth, even the intestines of a freshly slaughtered pig stretched across a young boy's face hanged for stealing fruit. But to behold your mask, the mask of a truly despicable human being, well, that is the most terrifying mask of all. It is no wonder the witch chose you. You deserve this most."

The eagle man stabs his dewclaw through the right side of my chest, shattering my clavicle, sending blood and bone shooting through the air. His claw wraps behind my shoulder, pulling flesh from tendons, snapping my wing from my shoulder. Unlike the eagle man, I am unable to reverse my form, trapped within the hideous cage of broken bones. He pushes my flesh into his mouth, gums gnashing maniacally, blood and strips of skin hanging from his face.

I close my eyes, rolling into a flap of human skin, and fold it around me like a warm coat on a winter's day. I think of the land around me, and how I had cut away the dead branches from the forest to build a fire, slicing them into small chunks with my sawhorse, digging the drainage channel in the front garden with my bare hand. I think of the bowsaw I used to cut away the mass of huge creepers the witch had said bothered her in the summer, lugging it outside, groaning as it grew back. I think of my concern as the top dam began to lose water, the earth shaly, yellow, and hard, and how the witch said not to worry, for the land always found a way to repair itself. I think of all the times I took the clippers to the hedge up on the hill and hacked away at the small garden, my arm straining with pain, just so the witch could see the full horizon as the fat orange sun went down in the evenings, the moon full and eager to please. I think of the gutters choked with leaves, the skins left to tan in the back room, the smell of rot I had attributed to dead insects choosing the corners of the windowsill as their final resting place.

I think of the witch and her magic. I think of her spells and her promises. She had died in bird form, her short, hooked beak dripping with blood. I had raised the gun. I didn't want to lose her, but I felt she was always too neat, too careful, too accepting of the world around her. I had wanted dark magic, hard magic, the power to transform, to transmute, to twist, to bend, to burn, to warp. I had wanted power, glory, fame. Everything life had denied to me. Yet, in my gluttony, I had overlooked her.

"Who did you rob?" the eagle-man shouts, flesh dripping from his teeth. He stabs his dewclaw through my abdomen, and I gasp in agony as I watch. "Tell me who, so, I can take your fetid body and dump it on their doorstep or hang your flesh from a tree outside their house for all the world to see and ridicule. The villagers will flay you like the animal you are!"

"The witch! I took them from the witch!" I cry, body trembling as the knotted vine pulls tighter around my throat. A long, thick black vine shoots in front of me. It twists around my leg, and impales my cloaca, shooting pain through my nerve endings, engulfing me, like a nail erratically stabbing my insides. For a moment, the world seems to stop. The vine pierces through my organs, hot blood bubbling like water in my mouth. It slithers up through my body, shooting out of my mouth. It wraps itself around my beak, ripping it from my face. Blood splatters and bone and flesh and keratin crack, crumbling together like a rotting peninsula. The vines wrap themselves around and around my body, entwining with my flappy flesh to become a second skin, the bones of my wing spread above me like the branches of a tree.

A single tear runs down the eagle man's face, his features contorted in a mixture of despair and pity. He leans towards me, so close I can feel his breath on what remains on my face, sharp and warm.

"You took everything from me," he intimately murmurs. "Everything. My soul is trapped within a host I have no control over. I merely exist in this foreign body, my every movement mechanical, rehearsed. Just because you are born incomplete does not mean you have the right to make others incomplete, too. You are heartless."

The eagle man bends down to the earthen floor and retrieves a small piece of skin, its rancid stench so obtrusive I gag.

The vomit shoots up from my stomach, pushing through the choking vine, lumpy and painful, until it lunges up my oesophagus and pours out of my small, circular nostrils, dripping onto the ground below me. He presses a chunk of white skin over my head, moulding it to form a human face.

He stares into my eyes, face gleaming with triumphant pride. "There you go," he whispers. "You are human again. You can die in peace. Now, I must go outside and deal with the hunter. I do not like guns. Guns are fired. There will be no fire in my gully."

I wish I'd retrieved the witch's bones from the water and buried her in the forest. I wish I had asked her what she truly looked like. I wish I had accepted myself as I was, a one-armed woman who only wanted to see the world. But I cannot. For she is dead. I am now one with the gully, and the gully is one with me.

SCARAB

June looked up at the mirrored ceiling and ran her fingers through her hair, tugging at the knots that refused to come out. She had installed the mirrors with the help of Tom, and while she had initially loved them, there was a coldness in the room, a strangeness in the room, that had not been there before.

She uncrossed her legs and lay on her back, resting her head on her hands. Her mother had disapproved of the mirrors, but at twenty-seven June didn't care much what her mother thought. The woman rarely visited her. Let her be spooked. She chewed on her bottom lip and uncrossed her ankles, then crossed them again. She winced at the pain in her bones, so brittle and fragile she feared they would break at any moment. Her friends called her an insect in jest, yet that was what June was. A long-limbed insect with a mass of knotted blonde hair.

June pulled off her shirt and shorts, staring up at her underwear. They were too tight and clung to her like a second skin, yet if they were any looser, they'd slide off. Her bra looked like it was made for children, covering her flat chest. She hadn't developed the way other girls had.

She thought of her mother, the woman drunkenly telling June she hated her life. She thought of the nights she had been kept awake, her mother forcing her to listen to her sad stories. All she wanted was a sense of control, to be able to stand up to the woman. All she wanted was her mother to see her as something more than a person to cry to. Was that so much to ask?

June frowned, watching her face contort in dismay. She lifted her arms and held her hands out in front of her, waving them around in the air. Her reflection mirrored her actions, and she grimaced, her arms too heavy to hold. They flopped on the carpet, and she rubbed her tired eyes with the back of her hand. She gazed back up at the mirror. Her eyes looked down at her in disapproval. A line of unpicked scabs lined her cheekbones, clinging to her face for dear life. She picked at them and flicked the dry skin onto the floor.

She ran her hands down her sides and wriggled out of her underwear, removing her bra first and then her panties. June looked up at herself in the mirror. Her once soft skin was stretched over her skull, her hair so dull and thin it fell out whenever she brushed it. Her knees no longer knocked together as she walked. A Christmas beetle crawled up her leg and rested on her stomach. She reached across to her pile of books and swatted it with a small paperback, then tossed the book across the room, flicking the beetle onto the carpet beside her.

June looked up at the mirror once more. She wondered what it would be like to be a Christmas beetle. The metallic scarabs seemed to follow her around, fluttering over to land on her shoulder, as if they had something to say.

A second beetle alighted on her shoulder to replace the one she'd just killed.

"What do you want?" she asked, her voice barely above a whisper. "Why are you just hanging around? Piss off and do your Christmas duties."

The scarab's little legs skittered over to her collarbone and up and over her chin, sitting on her nose. She wrinkled her nose, yet the beetle did not move. It seemed unfazed by her presence, as though June was merely a spot to sit on and contemplate life as a Christmas beetle. She looked up at the mirror once more and gasped. The scarab had become enormous and covered her entire body, making her look round and fat and ugly. She leapt to her feet and stared at it as it fell onto the carpet. It was small. Barely larger than her fingernails. She rubbed her eyes and pressed her hand to her stomach. She needed to sleep.

June walked over to her bed and collapsed on the mattress,

placing her hands behind her head. Though her fingers were bony, and her knuckles felt like rocks, she was comfortable this way, as she didn't want to sink into the pillow. She closed her eyes and ignored the groans in her stomach. Her organs felt like they were attempting to claw their way out, yet she couldn't give in.

The scarab, now small again, moved to sit on her forehead, and she opened her eyes, staring at the reflection above her. Slowly, June raised her arm to push the beetle away. Her hand hovered above it, and she exhaled a terrified breath as the scarab began to grow larger once more. Frozen in fear, she could feel the throbbing behind her eyes and the thumping of her heart against her chest. Her muscles contracted, her gut twisting like a corkscrew, burrowing deeper and deeper inside her stomach. Her mind turned over and over like an engine that wouldn't start. She lowered her hands and covered her eyes.

"There's nothing there," she whispered. "Nothing there. Nothing there. Nothing there."

June rolled over on her side, drawing her knobbly knees up to her chest. She pulled the sheet up over her body, breathing heavily in the stuffy cocoon. As a child, she'd been frightened of the shadows on the walls, and scared of her parents when they'd attempt to reassure her there was no such thing as monsters. She imagined they were in on it, that they had concocted a conspiracy, and it was they who had sent the monsters to terrify her.

The scarab grew larger once more and pressed its whole body against her, its front legs piercing her skin as it burrowed into her back. The pain was like needles that had been dipped in ethanol, and June howled as it dug its legs into her skin and burrowed deeper into her back. The beetle tore open her skin and crawled inside her ribcage, pincers scraping against her like knives. Its front legs elongated and penetrated her arms, stabbing through her skin up to her hands and jerking them like she was a puppet. Its back legs did the same to her legs, and wiggled them around, as though it was dangling her stick-thin thighs on a string.

Her throat was empty as June tried to cry out for help, even though she knew it was unlikely anyone would come to her rescue. She had isolated herself, keeping her distance in a tiny unit the size of a shoebox. She wished she had called her father for her birthday. She wished she had read over her sister's manuscript. She wished she had been good enough for her mother to hold her after her first teenage breakup.

June screamed as the scarab jumped up and clung to the cracks in her mirror, her body swinging wildly as though she were laying in a hammock during a tornado. Her chest and stomach seemed to fold in on themselves, so all she could feel was intense agony. It was worse than her self-inflicted hunger. Her bed seemed so far away she could hardly see it, as though she was hanging from the roof of a skyscraper.

The scarab ripped at her body, piercing her body, becoming part of her body, ripping off her skin so it fell into a pile on the ground. June repressed the urge to vomit at the mountain of flesh, clenching her fists as her teeth fell from her mouth and sunk into her skin. She gasped in pain as her hair fell out in chunks, pulling off parts of the flesh of her forehead along with it, so rivulets of blood fell onto the carpet below her.

She thought of her mother once more. The woman had given June a quest to find the son she had adopted before June was born. She'd interrupt June's studies, feed her scotch well into the night as she told June over and over again about how she found her mother dead one morning when she was thirteen, how she had turned to drugs, how June's father had been her saviour. Yet she had never once asked June how she was feeling. She had never once asked June about her day. She had never once asked June if she actually *wanted* a drink. As June hid from the woman in her bedroom, barricading the door with her chest of drawers, her mother would throw June's uneaten dinner at the wall, screaming at her crying daughter.

June looked up at her body and vomited, crying as the mess slid down the bleeding muscles that had hidden underneath her skin. Tears ran down her cheeks, the salt searing her face like fire. She was trapped, just like she had been trapped in her childhood home. All she wanted was to become something else, to be something other than who and what she was. To be human was to love. And yet the one person she needed to be loved by had never said "I love you". Why bother being human if no-one loved you?

"Go away!" she screamed, throat hoarse and filled with chunks of vomit. "Get away from me! I don't need you!"

The scarab pressed a pincer into her stomach, emptying it of the little food June had consumed over the past three days. The contents spilt onto the floor beneath her as the scarab crawled into her stomach, nestling comfortably as though June was its mother and it had returned to the womb. In her intense terror June somehow screamed with her whole body, her mouth rigid, fists clenched with blanched knuckles, her nails pressed so deeply blood spilled from her palms. Her mother's face intruded on her thoughts once more, crying as she told June that she wished she had never become a mother, that she wished she were dead.

"Why don't you love me?" June howled. "Why can't you love me?"

June let out a final guttural scream as the scarab became part of her body, its limbs taking over her own, its horns impaling her eyes, so they fell out of their sockets and rolled onto the floor. The scarab pushed up against her spinal column, so her back arched at an impossible angle, her knees twisting outwards, her elbows twisting inwards. And as she hung there, her bones breaking under the strain of her contorted body, for a moment, the world was still, her flesh a symbolic token of her private inner thoughts. *You are not human,* her mind whispered venomously. *You do not deserve to be loved. The world endures your existence, as did your mother. She never wanted you. You do not deserve to be human.*

Were June a real human being, she would have been able to break free of the curse that bound her. She would have been able to break free of the nightmare that currently assailed her body. Yet she did not belong to the world, nor her body, and never had. A single tear fell from June's eye as her scarab flesh hung from under her, from under the hard dome that had formed from her ribcage, the flesh grapefruit red and spongy, dripping bloodied juice like thick raindrops.

"June?"

June cocked her head at the sound of her mother's knocking. She'd forgotten the woman had promised to bring over her Christmas present.

"June, I haven't got all day! Your dad is waiting in the car."

Lungs screaming, June took a final breath as the scarab's head burst through her own, and yet, she did not die. Instead, all faculty she had of her body was robbed, as the scarab dropped from the mirrored ceiling crawled over to her bed, making a nest within her sheets, burrowing as deeply as it had within June's stomach.

"June? Here I am coming all the way over to your house to give you a present and you're not even here! Typical!"

June heard the screen door slam as her mother went back to her car. She thought of the woman at her fifteenth birthday, drunk and flirting with her friends. She thought of the woman on her eighteenth birthday, drunk and calling her boyfriend an arsehole. She thought of the woman on her twenty-first birthday, throwing a scotch decanter at her. *I wish it were you I'd given up for adoption instead of him!* And when June started slicing her wrists with her razor, her mother didn't understand what was wrong. She assumed it was a teenage phase.

June's breath clung to her throat as she thought of all the times she'd wished she could disappear. She'd wish she could transform into an animal and run away: a lioness so large she could tear her mother to shreds, or a beetle so small she could slip away and disappear forever. Yet she could not leave her younger sister. She could not let her be devoured by the monster that was their mother. June had dreamed of living in another world. She'd dreamed of living in another's skin. She'd dreamed of finding a place of her own. She'd dreamed of living by herself. June had dreamed of one day completing her life's quest by finding her brother. Of proving herself to her mother. She'd dreamed of leaving the world and all its horrors, even if it meant leaving her beloved sister. Yet she knew that dream would never come true. She'd never find the Eden she so longed to wrap around herself like a comforting cocoon. She'd never find inner peace within her body, and would always remain an insect, easily squashed under the weight of her mother's shoe.

June opened her eyes. Her face had split apart like a blossoming flower, its pointed petals reaching out towards the warmth of the sun. The flesh hung from her face, covering her eyes so she was blind. The scarab's limbs protruded from her forehead, cheekbones, chin, leaving only her eyes unscathed so she became one with the insect, and the insect became one with her. Once more she thought of her mother. As hard as she tried, June could not love another. Failed relationship after failed relationship had stained her heart. She realised, at that moment, that her mother's love was all she wanted. No-one else could compare. She was hungry, starving for her mother's love.

The scarab curled June's body into a ball as the last trickle of blood fell from her flesh. Yet she continued to breathe, dreaming of love without isolation. She did not understand why she was born into her body. She looked over at the wall of photos, smiling with her old primary school friends during happier days, her goofy grin plastered on her smooth, unblemished skin. The scarab lying dormant within her human form, waiting to break free.

"June!"

Her mother's heavy footsteps cannoned down the hallway. She reached June's bedroom and opened the door. June's scarab jaw unfused, her mandibles growing impossibly large. In one swift movement she impaled the woman with her pincer, pulled her to her chest, and swallowed her whole.

"Do you love me now, Mother?"

SENSES

Alison sat up in bed, staring at the tangled sheets at her feet. She looked at the bedside table lamp and realised she had left it on. There was the opened ziplocked bag, now empty, sat on the bedside table, still smeared with the crimson remnants.

The odour was difficult to describe. She was a teenager who cut her wrists and legs and collected the blood in a plastic sandwich bag. She would smear the blood on the pages of a book—her special book.

When she opened the book, a surge of wet, tarnished copper entered her nostrils, sometimes so intense she'd cough up half her lungs. After a while, the scent of old, dried blood hung around her like perfume, clinging to her clothes, her hair, settling under her nails.

Alison pulled herself from the bed and slid the book back in its place amongst the others, camouflaged within a sea of dark covers, of scantily-clad women with pale, outstretched necks. The book fit neatly, as though it had always had a place there, and forever would. She sat at her desk and took out her diary. Inside were secrets Alison could barely admit to herself, yet she left it in plain sight, as though inviting her mother to read it. Taylor laughed at her diary, said a woman ought not to have one at her age. Alison wondered if he believed a woman her age ought not to have secrets.

She dressed and left the room, walking down the narrow hallway, slipping out the kitchen door to the veranda. She crossed her arms, watching the foamy sea. Tumultuous and tumbling, it rolled about like an acrobat, sending the scent of salt and brine up over the dunes, and over the back fence. Alison had been born in the house, was used to the distinctive ocean aromas, knew the smell wouldn't leave her bones. Alison needed to inhale the sea, to taste it, to feel it caress her skin, wrap itself around her body; to overwhelm and replace the other scent.

She missed her mother. Weeks had passed since she had gone. Her mother had been an agitated woman, repetitive, anxious, forever furious at herself for all the little things she couldn't change. As a child, Alison had worried about her. She lied about her to her teachers, so they'd stop asking questions. She had wanted her mother to buy her bikes, clothes, jewellery, like other mothers did. She wanted her to make pancakes on Sunday mornings. And while her father did all those things, he was not her mother, did not smell like her, and never would.

Alison wrinkled her nose as the scent of her forgotten coffee mingled with the salt. She retreated into the little house, passing the amalgam of bookshelves, statues, mountains of paper, as she made her way into the small, dingy kitchen. She held out her hand to pick up the coffee mug but paused, recalling the hum of the microwave as it reheated warm milk when she was a child. She was struck by the *déjà vu* of her ten-year-old self pulling the same steaming mug of milk from the microwave, handing it to her mother. Alison couldn't quite remember what it was like when her mother had been alive. She only knew she had been another person, once.

She left the kitchen and walked back out to the veranda and sat down on the old cane chair, leaning back as far as it would allow. She closed her eyes. In her mind, she could hear the waves as though they pooled around her, could feel the cool water lap at her feet. She remembered reading books about handsome sailors, brave, bold, full of adventure. She had often stood on the veranda, looking for signs of sails, but none had ever come. No sailor had whisked her away on an adventure in the blue beyond. Her mother had told her to stop waiting for people to find her, to seek adventure herself, but it had seemed fruitless. *Why search for adventure when you wouldn't live long enough to enjoy it?*

Her heart thudded furiously against her chest. She retreated within herself, within her mind—back, back, back to a time when to wake each morning was not a sentence, but a blessing. Back when her father would wake her with a song.

Wake up, wake up, Alison. Get your rod. We're going fishing.

She sighed. The veranda was cold now; the day had drifted into dusk. Where had the hours gone? The crisp air gently caressed her bare shoulders, and she gazed at the fiery colours of the setting sun, the twilight swallowing the sea. Purple, red, yellow, and grey grazed the sky, swirling like marble. Her hands clenched into fists, nails drawing blood. Her chest heaved as she croaked and gasped, making her way back inside, bumping into the tallboy dresser her uncle had left in the hallway last year.

Slowly, she entered the kitchen.

"I didn't do this," she said to the empty air.

Several of her mother's most treasured Queen Elizabeth plates lay smashed upon the ground; silverware had spilled out of the cutlery drawers, with pots and pans littered among the mess. Old, unopened letters lay scattered on the floor. *Mrs Annie Lansbury, 3 Orama Crescent, Orient Point.* Someone had ransacked the kitchen.

Who did this?

Alison shook her head. The room was small, cold, and drafty. It did not have the luxury of the newer, open-plan contemporary kitchens.

"Is anyone here?" she asked, her voice thin. "Hello?"

She really didn't want an answer.

She wanted to lie down and rest or leave this forsaken place altogether. She remembered the period after her mother had died, when everything was pure bliss, and she had experienced the most intense and vivid dreams of her life. Her mind and body had become one, and although her voice had begun to slur, nothing and nobody had been able to cure her depression in any other way. It was the most intense yellow and orange euphoria she had ever experienced. Instead of watching the sunset, Alison had *become* the sunset, scales and all.

A door slammed in the distance. Her head snapped to the

front of the house, she braced herself for a fight. *Perhaps her father had finally come home?*

Her father had had a sort of elegance usually reserved to women. He often reminded her of a cat, a cassowary, or even a swan. He had poise, grace, and seemed to glide effortlessly instead of walking at an ordinary pace.

Alison first realised he was unhappy when she was sixteen. She'd thought of him as solemn, as he rarely smiled, even when she brought pictures home from primary school. As she grew older, she sensed a darkness in him she did not understand. After many efforts to console him, to get to the bottom of what was troubling him without asking him outright, she decided he was not like other people. Luckily, unlike her mother, he was not a monster.

Alison crossed her arms and left the kitchen, staggering down the narrow hallway. She reached the narrow staircase and ascended two steps at a time, letting out a breath as she reached the landing.

She paused. Beside her sat the tallboy, littered with family photographs. She'd knocked over one of the frames when she was ten and had blamed it on the neighbour's cat, constructing an elaborate reason why the cat was in the house in the first place.

Sometimes, as a child, she'd thought the house might swallow her up and devour her whole. Now the photograph was covered in a thick layer of dust. Alison doubted anyone had handled it in a decade. Her mother's eyes stared at her accusingly, her mouth turned up at one corner with a wry smile.

"The whole world fears one another," her mother had once said, "but you only fear yourself."

When she was thirteen, at the awkward in-between stage, Alison dated a boy who had said her mother was weird.

"She's always singing to herself, the same old sailors' tune. Does she even have any friends?"

She had always known that her mother was strange. In fact, she wasn't even sure she was a real person at all. She would sit in her room and read as her mother washed the same dishes over and over again, singing, and wondered if perhaps the woman was an abstraction, an otherworldly creature, a distorted imitation of her real mother. She rubbed her cheek as she stared at the photograph. *Who was this woman masquerading as my mother, Annie Lansbury? Where did she come from?*

Alison made her way down the hall, passing the rooms on the right, running her hand over the wall. She paused and pressed her hand to her temple.

She looked inside the room in which her mother had slept. No-one had entered the room in a long time, and it was always closed to the world; yet now, somehow, the door was open.

Alison stared at her mother's discarded belongings. She walked over to the mahogany wardrobe and pulled an old dress from a hanger. She held it to her nose and inhaled deeply.

She sat down on her mother's bed. Her room had lain empty for years, and dust was everywhere. Damp, blue-grey floral wallpaper wrapped itself around the room as if it were holding it prisoner. The lone window, sitting peculiarly high on the wall, allowed a slight gleam of moonlight from outside. Thick, colourless spider webs flowed across the room, perched in the corners of the ceiling, gently lining the bookcase. A small, porcelain plate balanced precariously on the edge of the bedside table, a forgotten, mouldy sandwich sitting on top. On the floor lay a rough, tatty mat, and a bundled-up sheet reeking of dampness and dirt.

Alison looked over to the walls, wincing at the faded stick figure drawings of her family, her own caricature donned with elaborate, enormous wings. *Was that how my mother saw me?* Alison wondered. *A caricature of a person?*

She sighed and thought about the past week, and the money she owed PJ.

"Should I kill myself?" she imagined the first stick figure asking.

"Maybe after Taylor tells PJ about her one-night stand," the other figure answered.

"Would they even miss me? Would the world miss me?" the first stick figure asked.

Alison left the room and tiptoed back down the hallway to the bottom floor. As she walked, she realised how dank and dejected the house had become. The house was silent, except for the intermittent creaks and moans.

Black and brown mould dotted the ceiling in clusters, evidence of rain seeping through the roof. The two thin windows, unopened for years, were covered in grime and dirt. Alison wondered if anyone would ever attempt to clean them. She arrived at the foot of the staircase and stood quietly, peering down below. She imagined stick figures from her wall crawling out of the wallpaper and yanking her into the shadows.

Alison reached the bottom of the stairs. She leaned against the banister, sweating.

She sank to the bottom step and closed her eyes as her skin broke out in a cold sweat, enveloping her in a frenzied state of panic. At first, it had been easy. *This isn't bad*, she'd thought. *I want to use. Maybe I'll sneak out. I will do it! My thighs are cramping, my stomach is cramping, and I am tired. If only I weren't tired, I could get comfortable. One week turns into two. I am cold. I am drenched in sweat. My teeth hurt. My ankles hurt. Two weeks turn into three.*

Alison leaped up from the staircase and ran out to the veranda. There was nothing but endless ocean and a deep chasm of impenetrable darkness.

"Hello?" she asked. "Is anyone there?"

She sighed again. Perhaps it was the age of the house. Old houses were cold, the strange scratching noises probably mice, the sound of running water likely a busted pipe in the walls, the clinking and knocking possibly the heating system. She hadn't been in the house for several years—it was bound to have changed since then.

She looked out at the ocean. It was still there, a memory she'd buried under everything and forgotten. There was no ugliness to the sea itself, but she couldn't understand why it hurt so much to look at it.

The beach was the same: the two flags piercing the sand, the lifeguards wandering from one end to the other...there was not much to look at in Ocean Grove. People in the streets didn't seem bothered by the low-hanging power lines, the endless stretches of road that led nowhere, the desolate bareness of the bush, the hideous shopfronts. They went about their day, milling around the pathetic markets with pathetic people selling their pathetic junk.

Yet everything was different now.

She did not belong in this place anymore. Her memories of scabby knees, of broken arms, of rusted scooters, of tyre swings, of cubby houses, of rules, of her childhood freedom, were far away, removed from this unfamiliar place, as though they'd never existed at all.

Another door slammed inside the house. Alison slowly turned around, but still there was no-one.

"Hello?" she asked, more loudly this time. "Hello? I know someone's there."

Homeless people, or perhaps inquisitive kids? The house had been empty for years, despite the fact she owned it. Her mother had left it to her in her will. Yet people could have roamed its rooms, claimed it as their own. It was not like there had been anyone here to stop them.

She walked over to the old shell that had served as an umbrella stand. Slowly, she withdrew one of the larger umbrellas and held it close to her chest, wondering if it was strong enough to defend herself against someone who might attack her.

Alison made her way over to the stairs, pausing at the bottom. She knew if she went back upstairs, there would be no return. Her body was withered, years of abuse almost obliterating it.

Back then, she had tried to deny the sweats, the shakes, the abdominal cramps, her nausea almost choking her windpipe, her muscles aching so much she felt as if she had run a marathon. The pain of her addiction had been so severe it had knocked her off her feet. It had taken a year of methadone treatments to get her back on her feet. And while a part of her knew she was swapping from one addiction for the other, she also knew she had to keep trying, lest she waste away, just like her mother had.

Taking a deep breath, she made her way up the thin stairs, placing both feet on each step as she ascended. She stared at her feet, their heaviness almost making her lose her balance. Finally, Alison reached the top and let out her breath, feeling her lungs empty with such force she doubled over. She pushed past the pain and continued, eventually reaching her mother's room. The door was still ajar, inviting her inside.

She poked her head inside and screamed.

The two bodies were purplish-grey, their lips tinged a pale blue. The limbs of one woman's body lay spread-eagled in the middle of the room, some of its loose, grey-blue mottled skin still intact, its ribcage and pelvic bones visible between slowly putrefying flesh. The other body swung from the ceiling rafters, its legs hitting the ajar wardrobe door.

The overturned chair lay on the dirty carpet. Alison stared at the needle still in the arm of the woman lying on the floor. She clutched at the inside of her elbow, almost feeling the needle for the first time since returning to the house.

Alison looked at the bodies. She raised her hand to her neck again, fingers pausing before they reached her skin. She repeated the action three times before allowing her eyes to linger on the body on the floor.

Alison hadn't realised how thin her mother had become, how chipped and yellowed her teeth were, how ravaged her skin was. The woman's hair had been torn out in clumps, broken nails entwined within the knots. She looked at the body hanging from the rafters. She had been dead longer than the woman on the ground. Alison placed her hands on her own body, opening her mouth to let out a scream, but nothing came out. She tried to exhale the air from her lungs, but there was nothing there. A hand came down on her shoulder, and she jumped, turning to face its owner.

"Mum?" she asked.

The woman nodded.

"I don't understand."

Her mother pointed down at the two bodies, then pointed at Alison and herself. "Who was this woman masquerading as me, Annie Lansbury? Where has she come from?" she said.

Alison frowned. "I don't know, Mum. I've never known who you are."

Her mother shrugged. "Perhaps I have always been no-one."

"I don't… None of this makes any sense!" Alison exclaimed. "What is this?"

"No-one understands."

"Where is Dad?"

"I don't know. He never returned."

Alison looked down at her body once more. It seemed to be her and yet not her at the same time. "I miss you," she said. "I miss the way things used to be."

Her mother placed her hand on Alison's shoulder. While Alison couldn't feel it, she knew it was there. "I do, too."

"Why is this happening? Why did this happen to us?"

"Sometimes people don't fit into the world. They try and try, but they just don't fit."

Alison nodded. "I gave up."

"We both gave up."

"What do we do now?"

Her mother stepped over Alison's body and paused in front of her own. She picked up the chair and climbed onto it, then clambered up onto the windowsill. She looked at Alison and smiled, then stepped into her body. Alison clenched her fists and gasped, looking down at her own body. She wanted to pull the needle from her neck, but knew it was too late. She dropped to her knees and lay on top of her body, positioning herself, so she melted into it, and she and her body became one again.

THE DOG

Jean often threw rocks at the dog as she passed it on her way home from softball practice. It became a hobby, and she was accustomed to seeing the dog every day without fail. Some days she would throw stones at it, small and unobtrusive. Other days she would ram it with her bike, cursing it when it managed to scamper away before she ran over its tail. Last week, she had failed her math test, so on her way home, she collected a handful of pinecones and pelted them at it as hard as she could.

"There it is, there's the stupid dog," Jean said to Tom, as they walked their bikes down Jean's street. "Everyone feeds it, but no-one knows where it came from."

Tom looked over at the dog. laying dejectedly in the shade, and nodded. "Doesn't look purebred to me."

Jean shrugged. "Well, it is. Someone said it jumped out of back of a truck that passed through town, but I swear it's purebred. They don't breed mutts as working dogs."

Tom nodded, and they crossed the road to stand beside it. "Look at how dirty it is," Jean said. "I wonder when it last had a bath. Probably back on the farm."

Tom shrugged. "Hasn't anyone called the pound?"

"Why would they? It's not like it would be any use to anyone. It probably broke its leg when it fell off the truck. I've been stopping by every so often to see if anyone has picked it up, but no-one has."

Today she held a heavy brick in her hand, which she'd swiped from the top of Mrs Murray's crumbling garden wall. The dog knew what would happen when Jean appeared from around the corner. He and Jean would lock eyes, and Jean would lift a thin brow, as if saying "Are you ready, punk?" and the dog would merely close his eyes and bear the assault without protestation.

The dog appeared smaller than his shadow, and he would sit under the thin lilac branches of the nearby jacaranda tree, burying himself in the dirt. When he rolled on his back, rubbing his shoulder blades into the dry leaves, his tongue would spill out of the corner of his mouth, and a big glob of saliva would hang from his jowls, swinging in the late afternoon breeze.

Sure enough, Jean stepped into the shadow at five fifteen, except this time she had a companion. The dog looked up at the tall, gangly legs, the patch of spots on the boy's face, and back down to the holes in his shoes.

"It never barks," Jean said to Tom. "Maybe it was hit by a car or something. If it were human, it'd be like that retarded kid in our class."

Tom laughed and dug the toe of his shoe into the dirt. "Does it ever move from that spot?"

Jean shook her head. "Nuh. It's been in the same spot for ages. Look at it—looks like someone's chewed its ears off."

The dog closed his eyes and inched himself closer to the thin, crepuscular ray of sun that shone through the branches of the tree. The sky had darkened to a hazy orange with streaks of purple sticking out from behind the clouds. An unruffled wind rustled the leaves of the tree, and the dog shivered, burying himself deeper into the dirt. He appeared to have dug some sort of hollowed-out pit for himself, and he shook his body roughly, his fur catching the dirt so it spilled on top of his back like a blanket.

"Are you sure it fell off the back of a truck? Who owns it?"

Jean shrugged. "Dunno. Billy told me about the farm truck. Maybe it's just some runaway mutt. I always see signs around of lost dogs, but have you ever seen a poster about a dog being found?"

Tom shook his head. "Nah. Didn't even know people did that."

"That's because no-one cares about dogs the same way they

care about kids." Jean snorted and tossed the brick from one hand to the other. She had played softball for three years now, and her PE teacher often commended her strong swing.

"Dogs are disposable, y'know?" she continued. "They're always breeding. Kate's dog had a litter of thirteen last week, and two of them died. Good riddance."

Tom nodded nonchalantly and tugged at the frayed hem of his school shirt. "What did she do with them?"

"Oh, I think she gave them away."

"Nah," he said, "the ones that died. What did she do with them?"

Jean shrugged. "Dunno. Probably dumped them in the river, but who cares? They're just dumb dogs. Like this one here," she said, and she kicked the dog in the side, sending it tumbling out of the comfort of its pit. The dog didn't yelp; it lay there, under the tree, staring up at the kids with milky blue eyes.

"I reckon it's come here to die," Jean said quietly. "You know how animals sometimes do that? They crawl under a veranda or go behind a shed and just die."

"My mum said my gran did that," said Tom. "She went out the back and sat on the old swing and just died. Old people are weird. And then they die."

"Maybe they run out of boring stories to tell?"

"Maybe."

The dog looked up at the pair and rubbed its head into the dirt, nudging its nose against the little stones and small pieces of bark. Its fur had flattened down around its neck so it grew out in all different directions. Jean assumed someone had once owned it, and that it had worn a collar, but that seemed like a long time ago. She threw the brick up into the air and caught it; it weighed heavily in her hand.

"Hey dog! Show us a trick!"

The dog appeared to frown at them, and it wriggled its nose, snot dripping in the dirt. Jean kicked a stone towards it and laughed as it struck the dog's eye, laughed as it yelped.

Tom rolled his eyes. "This is stupid. I'm going home."

Jean grabbed his sleeve and shook her head. "Wait!" She looked down at the dog, at the spit on its mouth, at the dirt and grime congealed around its eyes. Its face seemed to sag, and the scruff around its paws was matted in dirt. Crusty patches of mottled skin flaked around the ridge of its nose, and its eyes, rimmed in a line of dried yellow rheum, fluttered open and closed.

Jean huffed. "Very well, then!" She stared at the dog squarely in the eyes and lifted her arm. Suddenly the brick felt a little too heavy in her hand, and she hesitated.

"What are you doing?"

Jean smiled. "Do you dare me?"

Tom drew his brows together in confusion. "What do you mean?"

"How much? Come on, how much?"

Tom shook his head. "Leave it alone, it's just a filthy dog. What did it ever do to you? Come on, let's go."

Jean frowned and rolled her eyes. "You were the one who wanted to see it! I wouldn't be here if you didn't beg me to see the dog."

"Me?" Tom exclaimed petulantly. "You said it was purebred and that I could take it home and sell it," he said, nudging the dog gently with his shoe. "You knew my parents were having trouble with money and you convinced me this would work. I even told my brother." He huffed in annoyance and turned to walk away. "You're such a liar."

"Wait!" Jean grabbed the boy's sleeve, and he tugged it away. "Come on, Tom. We can go do something else if you want."

"Nah, I think I'll just go home. I told Mum I would mow the lawn. This is boring."

Jean catapulted the brick towards the dog's face, and it overturned in the air and smashed against its nose, causing it to yelp in pain. It hung its head and covered its nose with its paws. Tom, grimacing, bit down on his bottom lip.

"Still boring?"

Jean skipped over to the dog and picked up the brick, then moved back to stand beside him, throwing the brick towards the dog more forcefully. The dog continued to yowl and she laughed, bending to pick up the brick once again. This time she hovered over the cowering animal and began to beat the rock against the side of the dog's face.

"Stop!"

Tom grabbed Jean's arm and pulled her towards him. She scowled and attempted to yank her arm away, but Tom's grip was strong.

"What's the matter, sissy?" she taunted. "It's just a dumb dog. I'm helping it die."

Tom shook his head, his body shaking, and looked down at the cowering dog. Blood dripped from its matted fur, and its right eye had closed over. Its breaths were short, sharp wheezes. It stuck out its tongue and attempted to lap at the blood, its left eye glazed. Jean untangled herself from the boy and raised her arm, the brick hovering above the dog's head.

She raised her left brow and smiled. "It was gonna die anyway." Then she bent over and smashed the rock against the dog's face, killing it instantly. Once it was dead she continued to beat it, and it stared up at her, unseeing, its limp body rolling deeper into the ditch with each blow.

When Jean had finished beating the dead dog, she nudged it with her shoe and laughed. "Dogs think they're so tough with their stupid barks and their stupid sharp claws. But they can be broken, just like you and me."

Tom dry-swallowed his lump of fear and let out a deep breath. "Why did you do that, you stupid girl?" he shouted. "Who do you think you are?"

Jean snorted and ran her bloodied hands through her hair. "I'm like a blessing to that stupid dog. Like I said: it was gonna die anyway. I'm just doing it a favour."

She looked over at the houses across the street, at the empty verandas, open doors. The early evening breeze blew leaves across the street, and the crickets began to chirp, as if reminding the children in the street the oncoming dusk could not hold back forever. A tall boy sped down the road on a bicycle, and two kids shouted at each other from within a tree.

"But...the dog was alive," Tom protested. "You can't just go around killing animals just because you want to."

Jean huffed and turned up her top lip. "Who says? You? You're just a stupid boy."

Tom shook his head and ran his fingers through his hair in agitation. "Oh my god, you're so dumb! Don't you understand that everything is connected? The circle of life? We have to respect animals because they love us more than they love each other!"

"Oh?" Jean replied, smirking. "Who told you that? Your hippy mum?"

"*The Lion King!*"

Jean laughed. "Wow. I don't even know why we hang around each other. You're such a baby!"

"Am not! It's true!" Tom protested. "You're an idiot!"

He wrenched the brick angrily from her hand and kicked her to the ground, then leaned over her and smashed the brick across the back of her head. She rolled on her side in a slump, limbs akimbo, her eyes crinkling open.

Tom stared down at her in shock, his chest heaving. A bead of sweat trickled down his forehead, then down his nose, dropping on the ground in front of him. He clenched and unclenched his fists as a hot flush settled across his cheeks. Slowly, he extended his foot, and prodded the girl. She was unresponsive, her body limp. He bit down on his bottom lip, drawing blood, letting out a long sigh of relief.

Tom leaned down and scooped the dog up in his arms. He closed his eyes and held it against his chest, body gently swaying, and pictured the yellow splendour of sunshine, the crackling leaves of autumn, and the humming and chirping of spring birdsong. He hoped the dog had basked in the warm sunlight behind a racing river, had felt the cool spring air run its fingers through his fur as he lay upon a satin green hill, or had slumbered cosily beside the hearth inside a home with a family who loved him. He imagined the dog chasing cats always out of his reach, scampering down alleyways and dodging fast cars. He smiled as the cicadas' relentless cry pierced through his thoughts, and opened his eyes, a single tear running down his cheek.

"Come on,' he said, cradling the dog against his chest, as he walked away from Jean and the jacaranda tree, "let's go home."

THE TOWN HALL

The town hall, rebuilt last September, had been recently painted a bright lilac—Mrs Dawson's favourite colour. She and Mr Dawson lived next door, and, because of that, she concluded, they should be able to choose the colour of the building, for everybody else in the town lived in the village green and therefore didn't have to stare at the dilapidated old building every day like they did. Already, however, the paint had begun to peel. The residents of the town walked on the other side of the road under the dense canopy of mango trees, which protected them from the harsh January sun. However, everybody agreed it best to wait until Autumn to repaint the building.

Mrs and Mr Dawson sat on their veranda chairs and watched as the children filed one by one into the town hall, ushered in by their parents, some nervous, others jubilant. Mrs Dawson watched the proceedings every year as she sat on her veranda and clutched an old photograph of her young son. She missed Billy dearly. Her daughter, Marta, was a saint, of course, a beautiful woman now in her mid-thirties raising three children on her own. Mrs Dawson often took care of the boys when Marta travelled for work. She'd send them outside, to roam her back garden, out of her sight.

Mr Dawson ran a hand through his sticky hair, swatting mosquitos from his face. "Shall I make us some punch?" he asked.

Mrs Dawson nodded. She had dozed on her veranda chair for most of the morning, though she was now bright-eyed and alert as she watched the residents file into the town hall. She had joined the congregation many times, though this year she and Mr Dawson had not received an invitation. After fifty years in the small town, it was the first summer she could relax.

"Bring some cheese and biscuits, too, would you?" she called.

"Sounds good, love!"

Mrs and Mr Dawson spent a great deal of time on their veranda. They liked to watch the comings and goings of the town, especially in the hall, and lived on a particularly picturesque street. Although it was only mid-afternoon, the sun had begun to drop behind the ridge, the shadows approaching as slowly and steadily as a tide. The town hall sat in the middle of a gully—the town lay far away from the hustle and bustle of city life, seemingly closeted away from the rest of the world—and when Mrs and Mr Dawson ventured out to the ridge, they took photographs of the olive tree grove on the grassy rim, surrounding by overgrown foliage and dark, crumbly, rotten trees nobody had cut down. Sometimes, Mrs Dawson thought about going beyond the edge of the gully and into the grove itself. But she was older now. She hadn't the strength for adventures.

"Here you go, love."

Mr Dawson resumed his seat on the veranda, placing a small cheese and biscuit platter with pickled onions, gherkins, and canned mussels on the wooden table between them. He set the punch beside the platter. Mrs Dawson made herself a cheese and mussel biscuit sandwich and diverted her attention back to the town hall. A tall police officer in a crumpled uniform closed the doors, locked them, then stood in front of them, hand on his gun. His eyes swept left and right, and across the road. Then, once it seemed he was satisfied, he rapped three times on the door.

Mrs Dawson held her breath. "The doors just closed."

"I can see that, love."

"The police officer is on guard."

"I can see that, too, love."

"The reinforcements will be arriving any minute."

"No doubt about it, love."

"It's sweltering today, isn't it?"

Mr Dawson slapped a mosquito on his neck. "I knew we should have purchased the outside fan."

Mrs Dawson huffed. "The whole idea of an outside fan sounds ridiculous. What is the air for, if not to cool us down?"

"Um… To breathe?"

"Don't be such a smartarse."

"Sorry, love."

Around them, the air thickened. The front lawn, covered in dead branches, was a crackled yellow. If the sky hadn't been so clear, Mrs Dawson would have assumed a cloud had hung over the lawn for its whole growing life, as if it was not the grass itself that was dead but all the trees and plants that grew from it. The fallen boughs lay decayed on the ground. Mrs Dawson watched Mr Dawson survey the lawn and wrapped her arms around herself as an unexpected gust of chill air cut across the veranda with the suaveness of a blade. Within moments, however, the oppressive heat returned, and the couple both resumed their cheese-and-biscuit-and-mussel eating.

"Good gracious!" Mrs Dawson muttered, wiping her forehead with the top layer of her skirt. "That was bizarre."

"It's summer, love," Mr Dawson replied, stuffing his mouth with pickled onions and gherkins. "Soon, there'll be thunderstorms. I can smell it. It's not far off."

"A thunderstorm, eh?" Mrs Dawson huffed. "Bet it will whip up all those branches and toss them onto the veranda. I'm always cleaning this veranda, you know? Always. You never lift a finger."

"Come now, love. It's probably started."

Mrs and Mr Dawson turned their chairs to face the hall. While the doors were closed and guarded, they could hear everything and partially see inside through the three rectangular windows on the right side of the building. They had the advantage of being able to see into the building, and the knowledge that those inside could see out, which often made Mrs Dawson nervous. She couldn't dream of what the people in the town thought of them. She'd heard whispers in the grocery store from mothers about how lucky Mrs Dawson was to be excluded from the event, or how sorry they were that she lived next door to the hall, or how angry they were she didn't have to go through the ordeal again. While Mrs Dawson had friends, she understood their reasoning, and why Marta had moved away. Her poor daughter had been hounded for five years.

Mrs and Mr Dawson ate with trepidation swelling in their stomachs. Mrs Dawson was always ill in the summer. She usually put it down to heatstroke, but deep down she knew otherwise.

"What do you think they tell the children?" she asked.

"Huh?"

"The children. What do you think they tell them?"

Mr Dawson shrugged and ate another pickled onion. "Well, are they still taught about it in school?"

Mrs Dawson shook her head. "That stopped about five years ago. Now they just round them up without an explanation. I mean, I'm sure their parents tell them something, make something up, but nobody else does. What do you reckon they tell them?"

"Huh?"

"The parents. What do you think the parents tell them?"

Mr Dawson shrugged once more. "Don't know, love. Perhaps they add it to the curriculum. Like Math or English. A Social Science class. This is what happens. This is the day it happens. But I'd think they'd leave out the why and the how. Otherwise, they'd have to drag the children into the hall, and that would cause a great big mess, and who wants that? Nobody."

"Oh! There they are."

Mr and Mrs Dawson watched the convoy as it made its way down the street. The Humvees, while only lightly armoured, had been used for as long as anyone could remember. Once, they had no roofs, only windshields. Later, they boasted a fully armoured passenger vehicle with bullet-resistant glass. Now, the five vehicles had basic gun shields or turrets, necessary for the increasingly hostile summer. Many people had begun to protest inside the town, though few dared to do so outside the borders. Mrs Dawson had known several protesters who had left the town and never returned. While she liked to think they settled somewhere else, her aerobics class gossip speculated otherwise.

The vehicles stopped in front of the town hall. One parked

in front of Mr and Mrs Dawson's house, though neither of them moved to say anything. They had learned to simply observe. Twelve heavily-armoured military personnel jumped out of the trucks and surrounded the hall, relieving the police officer of his duty. The tall man with the crumpled clothes wiped the sweat from his brow and exhaled a sigh of relief, swiftly walking over to the parked police car and driving away.

"Well, then," Mrs Dawson remarked. "Weren't there only ten trucks last year?"

"Yes, love," Mr Dawson replied. He pulled out a little black book from his shirt pocket and opened it up, leafing through the pages. "Ten last year, eight the year before, seven the year before that, then six. Remember that unseasonably cold summer when there was only one?"

Mrs Dawson nodded. "That was before Billy."

"Ah, yes," Mr Dawson said, placing the book back inside his pocket. "I've still got his bike in the shed."

"I know."

"And his basketball."

Mrs Dawson frowned. "I thought that Robbie kid pinched it? Remember, when Billy was nine?"

"Hmmm…." Mr Dawson tapped his chin. "Nope. I think Robbie stole his soccer ball. I distinctly remember Billy having his basketball on his tenth birthday."

"Ah, well," Mrs Dawson muttered. "Can't always be right."

"No, love."

Mr and Mrs Dawson checked their watches. Mrs Dawson looked over the road again. "Later on, can you go down the road and get some flowers? Purple delphiniums, if you can. It's been roses after roses, and I'd like a change. Wouldn't you?'

"Yes, love."

"You know, I just don't know, sometimes. I just don't know." Mrs Dawson said. "You'd think all this barbarism would be quelled by now. Times have changed. The world has changed. There are more distractions these days. Less time for reading and real discussions. Sometimes, we just have no time for ourselves. That Linda always wanders around like a zombie in the chemist.

Always on her phone, texting. And Audrey, that young girl on the skateboard… Always taking photos of herself. She's a real danger to others, you know? Skating around with her arm in the air. Nobody ever talks to each other, anymore. Nobody ever talks."

"I know, love. But that's just the way, isn't it?"

Mrs Dawson rubbed the side of her face and placed her arm on the arm of the chair, resting her chin on her fist. The armoured men tapped their watches and signalled for each other to be on alert. Two short men and a thin woman spoke into their radio, then held up their hands, balled into fists.

"What does it all mean?" Mrs Dawson asked.

Mr Dawson narrowed his eyes and ran his hand through his thinning hair. "Well, love, the powers that be determine it all. It's not our fault we lost Billy—it's just the luck of the draw. It could have been Marta. We can't know how things *could* have been. We just know how things *are*. Maybe it's for the best Marta isn't in our lives anymore. Maybe it's for the best we only see the boys on occasion, when it's suitable for her. What good are parents, truly? We raise our children in this town knowing what could happen to them. We have our garden. Our cheese and biscuits. And we wait all year for summer. We wait for something that's over in one day and then wait a whole other year for it to happen again. I told you years ago—we should have moved. Billy would have lived.'

Mrs Dawson jumped up from her chair. "You know we can't do that. Not while we're on the register. Are you blaming me for what happened?"

"Well, no, but I *did* warn you."

"You were the one who said we should risk going away, even after his classmates were chosen. Billy cried and cried, and you said 'It'll be alright, Billy. It'll be OK.' You kept us here!"

"You always do this! Make me feel guilty!"

"Do not!"

"Do too!"

Mr Dawson glowered at his wife, tight-lipped and wild-eyed. He leapt to his feet, heart hammering in his chest as he waited for the sound that signalled the day was over. Not the signalling of night—the frogs striking a solo, ringing note in the gully river, the drastic thickening of the air, the evening sweats which rolled down the face like clots of custard—but the single sound that ended it all.

The shot came almost as a relief. Its sound, strangely attenuated, ricocheted around the entire street, ringing through Mr and Mrs Dawson's ears. Mr Dawson exhaled a soft gasp, yet Mrs Dawson was silent in her chair, an unsettling smile dimpling her cheeks. Mr Dawson lowered himself back into his own chair.

The couple watched as Mrs Lansbury ran screaming from the lilac hall, tear-streaked, hair whipping behind her.

"My baby! My baby!"

She fell to the ground in the middle of the road, hunched over, moaning incoherently. Mr Dawson rose to help the woman, yet Mrs Dawson held him back.

"We always take them in. Let someone else do it for once. Besides, no-one helped us with Billy, and we had to clean it up ourselves. Remember?"

Mr Dawson nodded and resumed his seat. "I remember."

The couple watched as a small crowd gathered around Mrs Lansbury, and one of the military personnel picked her up and threw her over his shoulder, tossing her into the back of one of the Humvees. The door slammed with a heavy thud, yet Mrs Lansbury's screams could still be heard. The driver sped off down the road, and everyone came out of the town hall.

Above, the dark clouds grew heavy with rain, and a sharp crackle of thunder shot across the sky.

"Oh, well. That's another summer, then," Mr Dawson said.

Mrs Dawson nodded. She stood up and leaned against the veranda railing, looking down at the people milling around the street. "Does anyone want cheese and biscuits?" she called. "We've got pickled onions, too!"

METAMORPHOSIS

"You have to make yourself vomit," Sophie said. "You have to do what you can to get it out of you. Feel it deep inside you, and then go deeper. And then vomit."

Her nails were painted cornfield blue and chipped at the end. William raised a brow as he leaned against the headboard, crossing his arms against his waist. The woollen blanket lay crumpled below his ankles. He looked at Sophie. She wore a ruffled cream shirt with a thin lace collar and black jeans that hugged her legs. Her scuffed boots were speckled with dry mud. William ran his jagged nail along his chin. Sophie was beautiful in a ramshackle kind of way. He loved her calloused lips, the way they felt as they met his. He loved her pointed chin, even though she said it was beastly. He loved the crook in her nose, the line of scabs along her left cheek.

"You can feel it here," she said, tapping the hollow below her collarbones.

"Can it really come out?" William asked. He had always been naïvely optimistic.

Sophie nodded. She leaned against the chest of drawers, absent-mindedly tugging on the left side of her collar. "Alison said hers came out without any trouble. She said it was ready to come out, and so it did."

"Did you see it?"

"Not in the flesh. But she sent me a picture. It was so strange. You know how things are so ugly they're beautiful? Like those ugly swans with crooked necks, so ugly you can't look away? That's what it looks like."

William ran his fingers through his tangled dark hair and wriggled down the bed, rolling on his side with his head in the crook of his arm. He and Sophie had met on their first day of high school. Paired in English class, they'd stuck together like glue. She had smiled when William asked her to lend him her pen; the following day she'd reserved his seat next to hers.

Sophie looked nothing like her sister. Annie was a beastly woman without any ankles or self-esteem. Sophie had always been the clever one. She had always known what people thought of her, what they saw in her. She'd been aware of herself more than others — the intricacies of how her clothes wrapped around her skin, how her skin wrapped around her bones. The awareness of her status as someone, some*thing*.

"What if it doesn't come out?" William asked. His voice had dropped to a low hush, almost indiscernible. He closed his eyes as his body folded in on itself in his mind, all its skin stretching, its bones gnashing together, the blood, the oxygen, the nutrients, the hormones, the carbon dioxide all jumbled together like a wild, untameable circus.

Sophie sat down on the end of the bed and leaned backwards.

"It *will* come out." Sophie said. "You just have to try. Just expel it out of you like you would vomit."

Nostrils flaring, William ran his hands over his forehead, bringing them down to cover his eyes. He bit down on his bottom lip, pressing his teeth on the flesh as hard as he could. "I don't understand it at all," he said. "We're brought up thinking we know everything about our bodies, and then one day they tell us the truth, and it's like we never really knew ourselves at all."

Sophie smirked. "You're very dramatic. You know that, right?"

"I know." William huffed a sigh and looked around the room. The bare bulb hanging from the ceiling was uncomfortably bright and flickered intermittently with the rhythm of a clocktower bell. Between the flickers the room felt as though it were moving. William expected it to explode any second. He frowned. He had known this room since childhood. Yet now, he imagined if he peered into the cupboard, so messy was his mind that he would not see his neatly folded clothes, but wreckage so untameable it would frighten him away.

William looked at Sophie. "This just seems so quixotic. Isn't there another way?"

Sophie shook her head.

He remembered shoving the toothbrush down his throat for the first time. He was fourteen and had cried, actually *cried*, after his mother drunkenly hit him. It wasn't anything unusual— she'd kept him up at night since he was a kid, telling him about how sad she was, how she had broken so many things in her life she couldn't put it all back together. But this night she had called him a "fat sack of shit", and he had locked himself in the bathroom and stared at himself in the mirror. *You are a fat sack of shit*, he'd mouthed, picking up the toothbrush.

"You've just got to be optimistic," Sophie said.

William screwed up his face in annoyance. "'*You've just got to be optimistic*,'" he mimicked. He didn't understand why it wouldn't come out. Everything else had. The dinners, the deserts, the late-night snacks. But the one thing he truly wanted to be rid of would not come out. Frowning, he pulled himself up and slipped off the bed, making his way to the bathroom. Sophie was elegantly thin, and yet he was grotesque. He didn't know what she saw in him. *Why wouldn't it just come out?*

"I'm scared," William said quietly.

"Don't you want to grow up?" Sophie asked gently. "Don't you want to be like everyone else?"

William nodded and swallowed the lump in his throat.

"Why don't you try now?" Sophie asked.

"*Now?* But you're right here. I don't want you to see me like that. It will be... I will be ugly."

Sophie smiled. "Ugliness is a point of view, William."

She leaned forward and kissed him on his bloody forehead. William looked around the room. It was messy. His school books were stacked haphazardly at the foot of his bed. His computer desk covered in yellow sticky notes. Posters, curled at the corners, hung on the wall with meagre bits of blu-tack. He looked at Sophie.

117

While he didn't have the same confidence in himself that she did, he appreciated her support.

William nodded resolutely. If Sophie could do it, then so could he.

He pressed his hands against his chest, ignoring the spasms of pain shooting through his body. He could feel it in there, waiting to come out. Slowly, he ran his hands up to his neck and began to massage his throat. He pressed his thumbs to the lump and dug his fingers into his chin, pulling at his soft folds of skin. It was almost painfully hot to touch, the way his fingertips felt as he held them over the stovetop, testing his resilience. The layer of skin fell away as smoothly as melted cheese, stringy and sticky. He thought of the way his mother layered lasagne with parmesan, so the cheese stuck to the roof of his mouth and wiggled its way between the gaps in his teeth. Had she gone through the same experience as Sophie? He knew she must have, but he could not visualize her doing so. His mother had always been a woman in his eyes. He could not imagine her as a girl, just as he could not imagine himself as a man. What would happen to his body if he never became a man? Would his flesh, his bones, be discarded? Would he be left to rot in his father's shed, surrounded by turpentine and rust?

"Come on," Sophie urged. "I promise it's not as painful as it seems."

William nodded and tugged at the flaps of skin that covered his cheeks, pulling it over his head as easily as a jumper.

Please let me be a man, his frantic mind whispered. *Don't let me be one of* them.

He shuddered at the thought of what he might find underneath. Why couldn't he stay a boy forever? It wouldn't be hurting anybody. He'd keep to himself. He'd hide away. Nobody would ever have to know.

He frowned. A part of him wanted to remain a child forever. He wanted to wrap himself in his father's old clothes and learn to whistle as he did. He wanted to learn to play the piano like his father did. But he would never be that man. He would never be the memory of happier times his mother so desperately clung to.

Yet he could not remain a boy.

William pressed his hands to his face. It was soft like his mother's velvet dresses. Soft like her lips on his cheeks. He knew what his skin felt like. He didn't have acne like his friends. He would run his hands over his body late at night, conjuring fantasies of having someone else touch him. Ever since he hit puberty, he'd been both scared and elated. Soon, they would be after him. But for a while, until they came, he could explore his body, stroking himself softly, then harder, his body accelerating furiously towards unexplored territory. The new sensations, new feelings, had been almost painful. He wondered what Sophie had thought when she first started to explore herself. Had she touched herself greedily as she tried to make herself vomit? William wondered if propelling it out of her had been a pleasurable sensation or pure pain.

"I don't know if I can do it," he said anxiously.

Sophie rolled her eyes. "Are you a man or a mouse?"

He pressed one hand against the hollow between his collarbones and the other against his throat. He looked over at the mirror on the wardrobe door. Perhaps it wasn't time. Perhaps he had to wait.

Sophie looked at him and huffed as if reading his mind. "What are you so afraid of?"

It seemed to be a rhetorical question. William knew she was goading him but said nothing. Instead, he stared at his reflection. The mirror showed an underweight child, eyes wide with fear. Taking a deep breath, he moved his hand back to his neck and pulled at the flesh at his throat. His stomach churned in a mixture of fear and exhilaration. His skin fell away in large chunks, piling on the bed around him until his face was devoid of flesh altogether.

It was as though his body had died on the inside. The ladder of his spine tingled as he pulled away the flesh at his chest and back. While he could find not a modicum of comfort in the act, his body pulsated in thrilling accomplishment. *You're doing it,* his mind said. *You're becoming a man. You won't have to fear being one of* them *anymore.* What flesh that remained on his body was as catastrophic as his thoughts. He had become a creature warm and damp, every nerve animated and throbbing with the rhythm of his heartbeat.

Blood and bone and skin and muscle tissue fell from his body. His bones twisted, breaking. Droplets of William's blood fell to the ground like spilt wine. He gasped as his mouth snapped open, then closed, omitting a foul stench, as sickly as wasted offal. The putrescine scent of musty mothball-smelling skin and discarded raspberries and pineapples left to rot in the midday sun hit him like a bat to the face. *This is me,* William thought. *This is who I am.*

Sophie gasped. She pressed her hand to her heart, beads of sweat building on her forehead and upper lip. As William stepped out of his discarded skin, he wondered if she had watched her own body transform in front of a mirror like him.

"Press your hands against your stomach," she instructed. "And then vomit."

William was exhausted. He wanted to lay down and rest. Yet he knew he had to do what Sophie said. He couldn't leave himself trapped in this half-transformed husk. He couldn't fail. He didn't want to remain a child forever.

Taking a deep breath, William pushed down on his bloodied, skinless stomach one last time, praying it would come out of him. The thick, bloodied ball fell out of his mouth and into his hands. No-one had explicitly described what would come out of him, but it looked like some sort of bezoar the size of a tennis ball. The aggregate of undigested body parts was a mess of unwanted eyes, rotten baby teeth, and swallowed fingernails. A stream of vomit and blood fell out of his mouth a few minutes later, pooling at his feet. He had never felt so sick, yet relieved, in his life. He had done it.

He turned to Sophie. She smiled.

"You are beautiful," she said. "Now, your new body will grow."

William thought of his mother. What would she say to him? What would his *father* say to him? He wanted to see them straight away, to rush to their sides and wrap his arms around them. *I am now a man!* He would say to them. *You no longer need to be afraid both of your children will never grow up! Look at me, mother. Look me in the eyes once more.*

He looked at himself in the mirror.

Streaks of vomit and blood ran over his chin, trickling down his throat. He stared at his watery eyes, shivering. *You are one of them now,* his mind whispered. *You can never go back.* What world was he now entering? The demon of adolescence was like a dog; it came when it was called. It obeyed without a second thought. And that was what made growing up so scary, William thought, his body would always come when the time called.

He looked nothing like himself. He was a stranger. For a moment, he did not know who he was.

"How long do I have to wait?" he asked Sophie timidly.

Sophie frowned. "It should have already started. When it happened to me, my new skin grew over my flesh straight away, and I was a woman."

Panic seized William's body. What if nothing happened? Were they already waiting outside, preparing to take him away? He thought of his old neighbour, Thomas. He had disappeared after his fifteenth birthday. William now wondered if it was because the boy had never grown up.

William began to pace the room, taking care not to tread on his discarded flesh.

"Calm down," Sophie consoled. "Just wait a moment. It'll happen, I promise."

William gritted his teeth. "Well, *when?* What's the problem?"

Sophie's eyes darted nervously around the room. William knew something was wrong. Sophie was intelligent and practical. She knew the natural order of things. And yet she seemed unsure of herself, which scared William more than anything else.

"What is *supposed* to happen?" William asked impatiently.

Sophie opened her mouth to answer, then screamed.

William looked at himself in the mirror. He had become a shrivelled, toothless creature, looking as though a wisp of wind could blow him down. Deep wrinkles seemed to carve a map on his now immobile facial features; his eyes, heavily lidded and weighed down with wrinkled folds, were framed by thick grey eyebrows, his chin covered in specks of grey and white whiskers.

"*What is happening?*" William screeched.

He stared at his rapidly ageing body. His father had described becoming a man in such an intense and grotesque way, that William used to find the simplest act of sweating disgusting. Then, William realised his saturated hair and the salty drops that lingered on his lips were like the kiss of life. It reminded him that he would one day become a man, that he would one day possess a body he could enjoy for years to come. He had checked for grey hairs as soon as he realised what they symbolised. When he was younger, and not old enough to possess them, the excitement of having grey hairs, of growing older, was enough to quell his fears of not being accepted. But now...

"Make it stop!"

Sophie screamed once more and ran from the room.

William fell to his knees, fists in his thick, white hair. He had worried about being taken away for not growing up. What would happen to him now? He looked more like a father than a son. He stared down at his wizened feet and saw the thick, bezoar-like ball of body parts. Gasping, he plucked it from the bloodied carpet and shoved it back into his mouth, pushing it down his throat. Gagging, William felt as though his lungs were slowly filling with water, as though there was no room in them for air. Breathing felt like there was a lead weight on his chest.

"Mother," he wheezed. "Mother, I need you."

You are a fat sack of shit.

An imagined life flashed before his eyes. He and Sophie finishing high school, going to university, getting married. Their careers. Their first house. Their holidays. Their children. He loved her, had always loved her since childhood. She had shown him how to outgrow his fears. He wanted to swallow her and hold her in his heart forever. He wanted to wrap his bones around her and protect her when she felt the world was too much to handle. In his mind, they breathed inside each other. He would offer her his hand, be the bones within her when she could not stand. Their teeth would be in the same mouth, uttering the same words: I love you, I love you, I love you. But now…

She doesn't really love you, his mother whispered.

William coughed on the bloodied ball, feeling the room around him spin.

She never has, and never will.

Heavy knuckles rapped against the front door.

He tugged on his snow-white hair, grimacing as he pulled out fistfuls intertwined with the soft tissue of his scalp. Layers of veins and skin fell away in his hands.

They were coming for him, he thought. They were coming to take him away. He didn't know who *they* were, but the terrible stories were enough to scare him. Did they have a register of people on the cusp of puberty? Had they been following him home from school, waiting for his body to change like the natural progression of the seasons? Or had they known he would fail all along? *I did not ask for this,* William thought. *Was I such a failure of a child to deserve this unrelenting torment?*

The hallway echoed with the second knocking.

William hunched over, wrapping his fleshless arms over his knees. He buried his head between his legs, slow tears running down his body, now dark red and spongy like the flesh of a grapefruit, dripping rotten juice onto the floor. The continued flickering of the lightbulb cast thin shadows on the walls, like hungry fingers reaching out to him.

The front door opened and closed.

Footsteps climbed the stairs.

William's heart screamed inside his chest.

"Mother," he whispered. "Mother…"

The bedroom door handle turned.

HAPPY BIRTHDAY, EBONY

Ebony pulls the blinds closed four hours after the party concludes. She slides down the wall and sits on the pale carpet, staring at her reflection in the blank television screen. The room is silent, save her quiet humming, and the scratching of unclipped paws at the door. She crosses her ankles and looks down at her shoes. Red, like the blood between her thighs, dry and cracked like her made-up face. She twists her fingers together like a pretzel, letting out a sigh. Jack would be home soon.

"Did you hear," Tom asks, "about the man down the road? He's just moved in. Dad says he's a drifter, and we shouldn't leave our bikes on the lawn. But he's asked the man to help with repairs on the workshop roof."

Ebony looks up at her brother, tall and imposing in the doorway. She crosses her legs and looks down at her hands.

"No," she replies. "But I heard dogs barking last night. I suppose they belong to him."

The dogs do not sleep. Instead, they whine in the night, as though tossing and turning in their dreams. All through the week, Ebony has pulled her shawl around her shoulders and clenched her teeth. She uncrosses her legs. She wears an old pair of Cameron's overalls. They often shared clothes, though Ebony has taken these overalls for herself.

"Did you have a nice party?"

Ebony grits her teeth, blinking slowly. "It was alright. Cameron and I listened to records for a few hours. We drank wine." She smiles. "He bought me a pair of earrings. See?" She pushes back her hair to show Tom the silver hoops pushed firmly through her red earlobes. "He pierced my ears himself."

Tom says nothing. Ebony knows when Tom is silent he disapproves of something, or someone. Sometimes, he doesn't talk to their father for weeks on end. She often wonders if coughing in someone's direction is a form of communication, and if their silence through words is some sort of competition neither of them want to lose.

"What are you doing for the rest of your birthday?" Tom asks.

Ebony shrugs. "I don't know. I was thinking about checking out the old station-master's house on Quarry Lane. The wind makes it sound like a banshee. Cameron told me that the house seemed to be actually speaking to him."

Tom rolls his eyes. "Cameron will tell you anything you want to hear. You're his favourite."

"Am not."

The house was enormous, sitting on tall stilts twice the size of anyone Ebony knew. One, it was canary yellow with stained-glass windows, but the age and weather had dulled the paint to the colour of vomit.

Ebony thinks of her brother. Cameron will tell you anything you want to hear. *You're his favourite.* She knows he manipulates people as easy as winking and wears different faces for different people. Cameron has a very old soul, and often goes days without talking, and then when he does speak, it's something mean or cruel to other people, but he is never cruel to her. She catches him staring at her while they read together on her bed, simply staring, as though he sees something in her she can't. However, despite his flaws, Ebony can't imagine her life without him.

"It's sad, really," Ebony continues, "that such a place has been left to rot as the years go by, like an elderly person being left in a retirement home. Alone."

"You think too much, Ebbs. Go away. Cameron says he has another present for you, in his room."

Ebony grins, excitement swelling in her stomach. She rushes into Cameron's room and finds her brother on his bed, dressed in nothing but a pair of ratty old overalls. He looks up at her from under his dark curls. While the rest of the family has blonde hair and blue eyes, Cameron is pale, his eyes the colour of chocolate cake. Some nights, when their parents are drunk, their father throws their mother against the wall, screaming: "Is he mine? Is that child mine?"

Ebony sits beside him, and he wraps his thin arm around her waist.

"Ebony," Cameron says quietly, "would you ever kill a person?"

Cameron's room is stuffy. The window doesn't open, as their father boarded it up after Cameron said he wanted to move out. The fan had been removed a few years ago.

"Would you ever kill anyone?" he repeats, pulling a cigarette out of his crumpled pack. He lights it, takes a long drag, and passes it over to Ebony.

"They'd have to do something really bad," Ebony replies, inhaling the cigarette. The end is wet from Cameron's saliva. "They'd have to be evil, or something."

Cameron nods and makes himself comfortable on the bed, pulling his legs up to his chest. He undoes the buckles of his overalls. A trickle of sweat runs down his bare chest.

"But what if you just felt like it? Does there need to be a reason?"

Ebony frowns, listening to the sounds of their mother quietly sobbing in the next room. "There always has to be a reason. You can't just wake up one morning and kill someone."

"Hmmm…"

Cameron flicks his cigarette ash on the floor and stubs it into the windowsill. "So, you've never just woken up and wanted to hurt someone just because you can?"

"What? Like kill an animal?"

"Kill a person, stupid."

Ebony shakes her head. "I don't know if I've been angry enough to do so. I mean, Mum makes me angry but…"

"When's the last time that batty old woman said a single word to you?"

Ebony nods. "That's why she makes me angry. She forgot my birthday."

"Huh." Cameron smirks and leans his chin on his knees. "Would you kill her for that?"

"No. She's our mum."

"Would you hurt her?"

"No. She's our mum."

"Would you…"

Ebony frowns and nudges him in the ribs. "Why do you want our mother dead?"

Cameron shrugs. "I don't. I just wanted to know if you would kill someone."

"I really don't know. Maybe if they did something evil, then I might imagine killing them. I just don't know if I could. You know what I mean?"

Cameron is silent.

"Why do you ask?"

"I think about killing people sometimes," he replies quietly. "I mean, I don't have some scary notebook filled with drawings of decapitated people or their guts spilled all over the pages, but I think about it sometimes. I think about killing particular people. But not you, Ebbs. Not you." He glances at Ebony, his face impassive. "What do you want for your birthday?"

"Just your company. Always. But Tom did say you had another gift for me."

Cameron smiles, sitting up straighter in the bed. He strokes the side of Ebony's thumb, then grips it tight, pressing his nails into her palm. Ebony frowns. He holds onto her hand firmly.

"Now that you're older, you won't leave me, will you?"

Ebony shakes her head. "I would never leave you."

"What will I do if you leave me? If you move away?"

"You'll take out your eyes and place them on my windowsill so you can watch me sleep."

Cameron smiles. He reaches into the pocket of his overalls and pulls out a box of tampons. "I can always smell your scent." He pecks her on the cheek and springs up from the bed. "Put one in, and we'll go and have some cake. I made the icing just the way you like it."

They don't go to the stationmaster's house. Instead, the day passes quietly, just the way Ebony had imagined it would. In the evening, they sit outside on the veranda, looking at the town. Their old, Victorian house sits at the top of the hill, far away from prying eyes. Cameron wraps his arm around Ebony's waist.

"I thought you had vodka."

"I drank the rest of it yesterday morning," she lies. The cool air rustles her hair in the wind. "I'm surprised you don't have other women snuggling into your arm. When was the last time you had a girlfriend?"

Cameron stiffens. "I have you."

"Yes. But when was your last girlfriend?"

"What makes you think I'm not happy with you?"

Ebony and Cameron exchange a silent look. His dark eyes look like coals in the evening air. "Don't ask me that again. You know it upsets me." He digs his nails into her arm.

"I'm sorry."

They sit together in silence for almost half an hour, until Ebony spots their father walking up the hill. A young man strides confidently beside him. He has light brown hair tied at the back in a neat ponytail and carries a rucksack on his shoulder. Ebony recognises him as one of the neighbours from town. *A portrait artist*, Ebony thinks, *or is it landscapes?* Cameron looks at her and raises his brow. They don't have many visitors at the house.

"Ebony," their father calls. "I have your gift." He gestures to the man as they reach the top of the hill. "It's Alexander. He's going to draw your portrait."

Ebony doesn't like him. She's seen him around town and feels uncomfortable when he smiles at her. He's wearing a blue denim vest over a long-sleeved shirt and black jeans. His shoes are too clean. Once, she'd heard him talking about her family to the woman who worked behind the perfume counter at the chemist, and she'd deliberately stood behind him, glaring at him as he turned around, and he'd almost jumped out of his skin. She doesn't want him at their house.

"It's too dark, Dad," Ebony says. "He can't paint my portrait in the dark. I don't want him to."

"He won't be able to get her features right," Cameron says.

Their father's face darkens. "Was I talking to you? Come along, Ebony." He clasps her elbow, and the three of them make their way down towards the house. Ebony looks over her shoulder. Cameron crosses his arms, then turns and walks down the hill and into town.

After the portrait is done, their father invites Alexander for dinner.

Their house is cold and dark. Once, it had been a grand manor, but it has fallen into dilapidated disrepair. Their father has slaughtered a lamb for dinner. Alice comes out of her room dressed in a short black dress, wearing knee-high boots and stockings. Ebony wonders whether her mother is insane. She often sleeps through the day and rises at dusk, greeting the night like a rooster would greet the morning. Her long brown hair is tied up in a bun. She's put on blush and mascara.

Since it is her birthday, Ebony can allocate everyone their seats. She places her father at the end of the table near the door, her mother on his right, Tom on his left. Cameron sits next to her without asking. She tells Alexander to sit across from Cameron and leaves a spot for Jack directly opposite her father. She wonders if he will be home soon, and whether he will bring her a gift.

"Tell me about this house," Alexander says, breaking the silence. "It's grand."

Ebony's father nods. "My parents left it to me in their will. I lived here, so my children live here. When they grow up, their own children will live here. It will stay in the family."

"Oh," Alexander says, "you don't hear about family dynasties anymore. That's interesting."

"We do a lot of work around the house," Tom says. "We have our own workshop. It's an honest way to live."

"And what about your family?" Ebony asks.

"We moved around a lot when I was a child, so I don't have a lot of family," he says. "I think that's why I like to do portraits. It allows me to catch glimpses of people I meet."

"Have you caught a glimpse of Ebony?" Cameron pipes. "Have

you captured her perfectly with your pencil? How do you capture her perfectly? With a big net?"

Ebony grins. Their father juts out his lower lip in anger, hastily cutting into his lamb. Cameron takes Ebony's free hand under the table, wrapping his fingers around her wrist.

"Do you ever feel like you're cheating people?" he asks. "Surely, you're not that good, otherwise you wouldn't be living in town. There's nothing in town. Nothing for you here. You should go somewhere else."

Their father moves to stand, yet Alexander clears his throat, nodding towards Cameron. "You're right, lad. There's nothing in town. Nothing but a great pub and fantastic people to draw. Maybe you should leave this hill of yours."

"Maybe you should draw someone else other than my sister. I'm sure she doesn't want you to capture her soul."

Alexander moves uncomfortably in his seat. "You're wrong. It's a photograph that captures souls, not the other way around. In any case, your sister chose to sit for the portrait."

Ebony wonders if Jack will come home soon. He was the only child their mother wanted to talk to. The only child she was affectionate towards. She looks over at her mother slowly chewing potato. Her movements are slow and precise, like a zombie.

"Actually, she didn't," Cameron says. A red flush brightens his pale neck. Ebony pulls her arm away from her brother, yet his grip tightens on her wrist. She thinks of their earlier conversation: *I just wanted to know if you would kill someone.* "She's my sister. She doesn't know you. You don't belong here."

"That's enough!"

Jack pushes the dining room door open, striding into the room. He is tall and foreboding like their father, with the same crinkle around the eyes and crease along his forehead. Jack likes Cameron less than their father does. Ebony remembers an argument they'd had about her many years ago, when they were both teenagers, and Ebony and Cameron had shared a room. Ebony wanted her own room, but Cameron wouldn't leave her

131

side. While Ebony doesn't like Alexander, she knows her brother is being childish and acting up to prove himself. She wonders if he is jealous of the artist.

Jack apologises for his lateness and takes his seat at the table. "Happy birthday, Ebony," he says. He tosses her a small brown package. Ebony thinks of the box of tampons as she tears it open. *I can always smell your scent.*

"Wow!" Inside is a small silver ring shaped like an ouroboros serpent. She slips it on her finger and waves her hand in the air. "Look, everyone. Look how pretty it is."

"A pretty gift for a pretty girl," Alexander says.

Cameron digs his fingers into the bottom of her wrist. It hurts, yet Ebony ignores it. She doesn't want to seem childish in front of Alexander. When she doesn't respond, Cameron presses harder. She looks over at Jack, who is staring at Cameron, his mouth a firm line. She knows he's aware Cameron sleeps in her bed. He stays away from the house as much as he can to avoid his younger brother.

"You know," says Tom, "Dad said you were a drifter, yet I think you're alright."

Their father pales. "I didn't mean…"

"Oh, it's quite alright," Alexander says. He leans forward, placing his elbows on the table. "I understand your suspicion, Greg. You don't know me. I don't know you, or your family."

"Despite our differences, I know you drew a wonderful portrait of my daughter."

"She was the most delightful subject to draw."

Ebony inhales sharply as Cameron's nails draw blood. She crosses her ankles, holding in her tears.

"Say, shall we all look at the portrait?" Cameron asks, his tone sarcastic. "I wish to see my beloved sister through your eyes."

Ebony hates the portrait. She looks small and thin and pale. Today, she is twenty-six, but the portrait makes her look like a little girl. Her dark hair looks lank and greasy. Her cheeks look sallow. Her brows are too thin. Her father beams, praising Alexander's talent. Her mother smiles and suggests they hang the portrait in the hallway for everyone to see. Ebony wants to burn it and tell Alexander to go away. She hadn't invited him to her birthday.

"Thank you," she replies quietly, not meeting Alexander's eyes. "I must look very different through your eyes."

Jack stares at her, then turns his gaze on Cameron. Ebony knows he is aware of Cameron's possessiveness. She assumes he is aware of Cameron's nails in her skin. He's seen Cameron hurt her many times in the past. Yet he is silent.

After dinner and cake, Ebony excuses herself from the table. She thanks Alexander once again and kisses her mother and father goodnight. She hugs Jack tightly, and he promises to take her shopping in town in the morning. As soon as she puts on her pyjamas and gets into bed, she rolls onto her stomach and cries.

Ebony's stomach churns as she stares at the windowsill in her room. She stands there for what feels like hours, feeling the moon's gaze upon her. It is cold and dark, and her blankets are thin. Finally, she gets into bed and pulls the blankets up to her chin, staring at the ceiling. When they were younger, Cameron had etched their names next to the light bulb, and she looks at them now, faded and dull. Like her house. Like her birthday. Like her life. Sometimes, she thinks about moving away, but she knows she cannot leave Cameron. Her father is a reputable man in the little town, and the owner of a small business. He is distinguished and regularly has lunch with the council mayor. Ebony rolls onto her side, thinking of the bruises Cameron accumulated over the years. For a long time, she assumed he was clumsy, and insisted he hold her hand so he could steady himself as they walked down the street. Sighing, she reaches under her pillow and withdraws the half-empty bottle of vodka, gulping it so fast her stomach hurts. For a moment, the world spins around her.

"Ebony."

Cameron opens the bedroom door and comes into her room. He pushes her over to the side of the bed and slips under the blankets. She runs her fingers through his hair. He feels sweaty. His face is sticky.

"What have you been doing?" she whispers.

His heart pounds against his chest. Ebony wonders if he's been out for a run.

"I did it for us, Ebbs," he says.

"Did what for us?"

"I have to show you. This is a better gift than anything else I have ever given you."

Ebony shivers, though she is not cold. "But I appreciate your gifts. I know we didn't do everything we planned, but it was great nonetheless."

Cameron hums. "But it's not enough. So, I made it better for you." He nuzzles her head into her neck, running his tongue up under her ear. His lips close around her earlobes, and he unclasps the back of the earrings with his teeth. They fall onto the pillow beside her.

"Come and see."

Cameron pulls Ebony out of bed, and they hurry down the dark hallway towards the front of the house. Ebony stares at her mother as she sits smoking on a wooden chair beside the kitchen window, tears spilling down her cheeks. She doesn't move as Cameron unlocks the door and drags Ebony outside. The air is old. Ebony shivers as Cameron tightens his clasp on her wrist.

"Let go of me," she hisses. Cameron holds her tighter. "I said let go."

"Shut up. You'll ruin your present. I went to a lot of effort to make it for you. You're going to love it, I swear." He pulls her outside into the yard, and over to their father's workshop. Cameron isn't allowed inside, as their father thinks him a nuisance with tools. Only Jack can use their father's tools. Nevertheless, Cameron pushes the door open and releases Ebony's wrist.

"This is the man you'd dare leave me for?" he shouts. "This man?"

The dogs lap up the blood as it drips from above like raindrops. Cameron places his hand over Ebony's mouth as she screams. Alexander's naked body hangs from two hooks their father used to lift cars as he repaired them. The skin from his back is pulled up and over his head and eyes.

"Now he cannot see you."

His body is still pink. Ebony's face is carved into Alexander's stomach, so deep the wounds are more like chasms than slashes.

"Very few artists can do this," Cameron says. "There's a certain depth to carve the skin, and Alexander's unskilled hand would most likely get it wrong. He'd injure someone's nerves. Just thinking about his lack of talent makes me sick. How dare he defile you that way? Does he not see you the way I do?" Cameron chuckles. "Oh, I've captured him perfectly."

Ebony freezes, her body unable to respond to the horrendous sight before her eyes. She drops to her knees, screaming into her hands. Cameron pulls her hair and forces her to her feet, pressing his nose against hers. She vomits up dinner and her birthday cake, gasping as chunks of carrot try to expel themselves out of her nose. Coughing, she closes her eyes, desperately clawing at Cameron's face.

"You cannot leave me, Ebony," he says, kissing her full on the mouth. He licks the vomit from her lips and swallows it. Tears fall down Ebony's face. "Jack will do it again," he says through gritted teeth. "Jack will always do it. He goes away and comes back and then I am nothing. He destroys me, Ebbs. He holds me down and pushes himself so hard inside me I bleed. And you dare think about leaving me? You belong with me. I love you, Ebony. Don't you love me, too?"

Ebony stares at the flailed artist, his skin opened like wings. His flesh is dark red and spongy, like the flesh of a grapefruit, dripping bloodied juice onto the floor below him.

Cameron presses his mouth to Ebony's ear. "What will I do if you move away?"

It is almost impossible to speak. Ebony gasps, her body shaking. She wonders if she'll pass out. "You'll take out your eyes..." she stutters "...and place them on my windowsill...so you can watch me sleep."

Cameron wraps his arms around her, engulfing her with his body. He breathes in her hair, her scent, *her*, and sighs contently.

Slowly, he sucks on her earlobe, tongue twirling her earring.
   "Happy birthday, Ebony."

SYNTHETIC

Jack stood in front of the bathroom mirror inspecting his baby-smooth face. Not a hint of a whisker, nor a frown line. He ran his hands over his cheeks, searching for a lump or a scratch to mark his face, but he found nothing. He had never been scratched, bruised, or wounded in any way. He ran his fingers down his throat, drawing soft circles over his chest. No definition. No raised areola. Nothing. He stared at the shiny new straight-edged razor sitting in the toothbrush holder his father had given him for his birthday.

Frowning, he pulled down his underwear, pressing his hands on the inside of his thighs, and slowly moved his hips from side to side. He knew from the boys at school there should be something there. He was aware, from the sexual education classes, something should have descended by now. But the only thing between his legs was a hollowed crevice from which he urinated, deep and wide and mysterious.

Gulping a deep breath, Jack reached inside the crevice, running his hand along the walls of his body. It was the same smoothness of his cheeks, but warmer, supple. With one hand steadying himself on the sink, he bent forward and probed deeper, his fingers grasping nothing but hot air.

His skin, which had always felt cold and uninviting, was now warm and velvety soft. As a young boy, he had never touched himself but knew his body beckoned, daring him to uncover its secrets, to lure him with dreams of intimacy he did not understand. How long would it take for him to develop? Why didn't he look like the other men in the late-night movies his father encouraged him to watch? "When will you get a girlfriend, boy? How will you know how to kiss a woman? You need to grow up."

Jack was trying to grow up. He was. His father forced him to play football, even though he was smaller than his peers. His father forced himself to watch action movies, even though he didn't have hair on his chest like their muscular stars. He'd even once attempted to shave his face, to propel his body into adolescence. Still, nothing but open wounds that quickly healed. Sometimes, he felt like nothing.

Then, for the first time, he felt something hard.

Jack wrapped his fingers around the cold, metal structure. He ran his fingers along its six-pointed sides, and he conjured up an image of a cube in his mind. As he touched each point, he felt a shiver of pleasure run up his spine.

Jack gasped, quickly withdrawing his hand.

He considered his reflection the mirror. He listened for outside noises. Nothing. Jack knew his father would be home soon. Shoes off, feet on the table, beer in one hand. His father liked to poke fun at him for his lack of facial hair. "You're seventeen, boy! You look like you're twelve!"

Sighing, Jack pushed his hand deep inside himself, wincing at the forcefulness of his adventurous fingers. Teeth clenched, he drew a sharp breath as the crevice tightened around him, encasing his hand. Heart thumping, his fingers stiff, he tried to pull his hand out, but his body tightened as he pulled, and his heart felt like it would burst through his chest. He squeezed his hand around the metal structure, fingers slipping on the moist, pointed sides.

"Come on, come on, come on!"

With one last, forceful tug, the metal cube shot out of his body, flecks of flesh and blood spitting out with it, splattering the mirror, the bath, and the dirty tiled floor. His legs collapsed beneath him, and his head hit the tiles with a dull thud. Momentarily dazed, he pushed himself up, muscles aching as he watched the warm dark blood pour from his body.

Jack opened his mouth to scream for his father, but no sound escaped his lips. What would he say? How would he explain his grotesque, bloodied body?

"Mum…" The word left his lips like a whisper. "Mum…help… me."

Chest heaving, he reached for the metal cube, weighty in his small, shaking hands. He wondered if all boys discovered cubes inside themselves, and assumed he was just late to footy. What would his friends say if he mentioned such a thing? Would they be jealous? Or mock him for entering puberty last?

Jack wondered what the metal structure could be. In science class, his teacher had said the human body was a machine with joints, muscles, skeleton, propelling the force and motion required for bodies to move efficiently and effectively. Jack's teacher had told the class if humans didn't have joints, everyone would look and move like robots. "But it's hard to say these days," his teacher had said, "because robots look more like humans every day."

"Jack? Are you in there? Where's my fucking beer?"

Jack stiffened. His father was home.

For three long years, Jack had mourned his mother. In a sea of black and white, he mourned her scent, her touch, her warmth. While she had died when he was eight, and he told himself that boys don't cry, he remembered, quite vividly, staring into the same mirror wishing he had tears to shed. He wished he could freeze his mother and himself in time. But cancer struck suddenly and sharply. It rusted the body, leaving it nothing but an empty husk. His father had suffered, indeed, but his alcoholism had taken over, until Jack could barely recognise him. He was a stranger to him.

Jack lifted the metal cube to his eyes. He could find no crevice on its obsidian surface. Was his body different to his mother's? Would he get cancer one day?

"I spoke to the footy coach for you," his father yelled from the other side of the bathroom door. "You're starting next week! No boy of mine is going to stay scrawny and weak, you no-hoper!"

Jack ignored his father, running his tongue along his gritted teeth. They were slimy. He needed to brush more often. His stomach growled.

"Are you coming out? What the hell are you even doing in there? Jack? Footy's starting. Get your lazy ass out here."

Jack cleared his throat. "I'm here."

"Come and watch footy, Jack!"

"In a minute!"

Goose pimples flared upon his skin, and he shivered, his knees shaking. He pulled himself across the tiles, sitting in the tight space between the bathtub and the sink. For once, he was glad he was small. He felt safe in the enclosure, protected. He looked down between his legs. Blood poured out slowly, little chunks of metal entwined within the thick fluid. Without warning, he hunched over and vomited up tiny coils of wire. Jack dug his nails under the edges of the cube, prying the sides open with the last of his strength.

He gasped.

Inside were two round balls of flesh, one slightly bigger than the other. They were covered in a thin membranous substance, pliable and ductile. Jack squeezed one in his hand, feeling a hard, miniature metallic cube inside it. A cube within a cube?

"Suit yourself! No beers for you, pussy! Go back to your books and your dragons. Fucking stupid fantasy shit."

Pussy.

"I'm sick of you making fun of me."

"What'd you say to me?"

Jack cleared his throat, raising his voice. "I said I'm sick of you making fun of me!"

His father was silent. A few moments passed. "Jack, you've got to grow up and learn to brush the dirt off your shoulder!" he shouted, words slurring. "Take your cousin Alex, for instance. He's on the football team. He swims. He kayaks. He hangs out with his mates. What mates do you have, huh? When have you ever mentioned a mate? What are you, a fairy? I'm just trying to toughen you up, son. You're fucking useless!"

"You know what, *fuck you!*" Jack shouted, eyes wide as he stared at the balls of flesh with incredulous intensity. "You and everyone else can go to hell!"

"You can go to hell, you snot-nosed, no-balled twat! You never appreciate anything I do for you. I go to work. I put food on the table. And what do you do? Treat me like a slave. You won't even have a beer with me. What a joke. Your mother would be disappointed."

Jack gasped, stomach dropping. "Stop trying to change who I am! I'm not like you and never will be!"

His father got up off the lounge. Jack heard his heavy footsteps, the stagger in his step.

"Get your arse out here, boy! You need to learn some respect. Don't make me get the belt."

Jack froze. His father pushed open the bathroom door, cheeks ruddy, beer in hand. His face fell as he stumbled backwards. staring at Jack's mutilated body.

"I have balls!" Jack screeched, pulling himself to his feet. He stood in the middle of the bathroom. A sudden surge of strength flowed through him like an electric shock. He took a step forward, body shaking. "I don't want to watch the footy with you." He took another step forward. His father stepped backwards. "I don't want to play football at school. I don't want to drink. I don't want to fight. I don't want to watch stupid late-night pornographic movies with you. I don't want to do any of those things!"

Jack clenched his left hand around the soft, sponge-like balls of flesh. He clenched his right hand around the open cube.

"I don't want to cook a barbeque." He took another step forward. His father stumbled back, steadying himself on the hallway table. "I don't want to cook a camp fire. I don't want to catch a fish. I don't want to throw a punch. I don't want to take a punch to prove I am 'manly' and strong."

"Jack…what…' His father raised his hands defensively. "Holy hell."

"I don't want to change a car tyre. I don't want to ride a motorbike. Stop telling me to sleep with a girl. Stop telling me to be a man! I am not a man!"

Jack held the balls of flesh to his bleeding crotch. Glancing to the sink, he reached into the toothbrush holder and pulled out the straight-edged razor.

"Son, give me the razor…" He stared at the cube, yet he didn't appear perturbed. His eyes blazed with familiarity. He knew what it was. He knew what he was.

Jack wondered if his mother would have accepted him, had she still been alive. He wondered if she'd hold him and tell him everything would be alright. Jack missed her warm arms around him, her thin fingers slowly running through his hair. He missed the light touch of her kisses on his skin. *You're such a special boy. Perfect the way you are, since the day they gave you to me. I love you.* She had always read him stories. *Pinocchio. The Wizard of Oz. If I only had a heart, if I only had a brain.* Jack thought of his father's playful punches. His snide remarks about Jack's lack of facial hair. *You're such a baby. You're fifteen years old. I'm ashamed to call you my son.*

He slashed the razor in the air. Jack's father dodged sideways, tripping over the bath mat. He clutched at the shower curtain. However, the rings collapsed, and he and the curtain fell into the bathtub, knocking his head against the tap. Jack stood beside the tub, looking over his father, small and pleading.

"Give me the damn razor!"

"You want it?" Jack shouted. "Come and take it!"

"Son…you're not well. Your mother, when she couldn't conceive, we tried everything…"

"What?" Jack froze, arm shaking. "What are you talking about?"

"Your mother," his father rasped. "She couldn't conceive. We tried. We did. But it didn't happen. So, we adopted you, and then she died. I blame you, you shit. But I knew you were rotten the day they gave you to us. She didn't even want you. But I insisted. And she grew to love you."

Chest heaving, Jack's hand shook as he stared at his father, cowardly curled in the bathtub. He thought of his mother. Of her soft hands. Her warm, comforting chest. Her gentle kisses. Had it all been a lie?

"You're a horrible person!" Jack roared, waving the straight-edged razor around. "You just wanted me to grow up. But I can't grow up. Can't you see that? You push, and you push, and you belittle me and make me feel inhuman. Look at me! I *am* inhuman! But you're my father. You're supposed to love me."

He held the membranous skin to his crotch, staring at it with incredulous curiosity. Was this what the boys in his class saw when they looked down at themselves? As they plucked and poked at their tuft of coarse hair?

"Your father? No, no, no, no, no. You…you're an abomination!"

Jack stabbed the razor into his neck. His father looked up at him from the bathtub, jaw open. Jack stood still, his body unresponsive to the pain. He did not shed a tear. Heart racing, he pulled the razor out of his neck and slashed his throat from left to right. Blood dripped from the wound slowly, as though pulled by a lever. He'd expected it to splatter against the shower curtain, but it only trickled out of him, like water slowly making its way down a calm river. He'd expected pain. He'd expected tears. He'd expected to die.

"What. Am. I?" Jack bellowed, spittle flicking out of his mouth. "Tell me!"

His father shook his head, pale and trembling. He bit down on his bottom lip, slowly shrugging his shoulders. "I don't know! You're… What did the scientist say? Subhuman. Posthuman. Antihuman… I can't fucking remember! We adopted you." His voice wavered as his eyes bulged in terror.

"That's right!" Jack spat. "You don't know anything. You never have. You've never appreciated me, even as a child. But do you know what? You're the inhuman one."

Jack plunged the razor into his neck, repeatedly stabbing and slashing and cutting and spearing as hard as he could. He thrust the razor into his chest, twisting it around as hard as he could. Nothing happened. Instead, the razor hit a hard metal box where his heart should be.

Gasping, he stumbled into the bathtub, kneeling over his father, whose body had frozen still, his hands raised in defence. Jack pushed the razor down with all his strength. His father's face paled. Blood spurted out of his chest. He closed his eyes. His body went limp. Then, he was still.

Jack collapsed, his body intertwined with his father's. He

stared at the roof. *You're such a special boy*, his mother whispered. *Perfect the way you are, since the day they gave you to me.* Jack closed his eyes, imagining himself in his mother's warm embrace. *I love you.*

He smiled. "I love you too, Mum."

ANDROMEDA

1

It wasn't until we were about to enter the atmosphere that I realised Earth was a wondrous living, breathing organism. Looking down from the shuttle, I had an overwhelming feeling of love for my home. And Earth was suddenly not just my home. It was a planet, it was my planet, and it was alive.

It looked like a giant blue marble with white swirls, the kind you kept protectively in a velvet purse as a child. I could see patches of brown, green, yellow, and white, and while I knew I was looking at land, at water, at clouds, at ice and snow, everything appeared overwhelming. Why were there patches of green in those exact spots? What would happen if the yellow disappeared?

I had decided to become an astronaut when I was twelve years old. As a child, my dad would cook barbeques, and late at night he would tell me about the planets, the stars, about Earth. He would explain to us that Earth was exactly where it needed to be for humans to survive. That the Earth was just right: it was warm, but not too warm, it had water, but not too much. Just like Goldilocks, I had joked. Dad had laughed and agreed with me. Just like Goldilocks.

We had been at the International Space Station for six months, which was the usual stint: Olga, Serj, and I. Olga Kononenko and I were cosmonauts, and Serj Lindgren an Armenian European Space Agency astronaut. Luckily, we all got along, thanks to our communal love for bad television and science fiction stories. Entering the atmosphere was exhilarating, yet terrifying at the same time. Everything was red. Streaks of gold flashed by, so quickly I was sure I would have missed them had I blinked. The world was gorgeously dark. And then, it turned white, and then blue, and suddenly I could see formations of land and my heart thumped against my chest. I felt as though I had just come out of life-threatening surgery. I laughed, and Serj slapped my back in excitement. Olga grinned like a child and pumped her fist in the air, Bender style. I rubbed my temple in a mixture of exhaustion, relief, and exhilaration. We were home.

2

Reaching Earth was terrifying and violent. I felt more scared than when I'd first looked at Earth from space itself. The noise was so overwhelming I thought I would go deaf. And then everything was silent, everything was still.

Nobody came to greet us when our shuttle arrived at the Canberra Deep Space Communication Complex. It appeared the entire facility was abandoned.

"Where is everyone?" Olga asked, wiping the beads of sweat from her face.

I shrugged. "I have no idea. Perhaps there's been an emergency. There's no-one else scheduled to re-enter today, right?"

She shook her head. "Not that I know of. I'm pretty sure we were the only ones in orbit. There's the Land Rover on Mars."

Serj returned to the ship. Minutes later he came back and held up his hand. "No radio signal. Just static."

"How can that be?' I questioned incredulously. 'We made contact last week. Green light."

"I don't know."

The situation was baffling. We decided to stick to regulation and routine. Returning home from space was always an incredible ordeal. Instead of being orbiting humans of steel, we were all now broken beings who needed healing from the effects of microgravity. Since there was no-one to aid us, we had to do it all ourselves.

Everything in my body felt heavy, especially my limbs, and

my mouth. We all hadn't realised we had learned to talk with weightless tongues—everything had occurred so naturally over time—and now, we had to decompress.

"Gosh, my eyes are sore," complained Olga, as she vigorously windmilled her arms. I nodded in agreement.

"It'll pass. Where the fuck is everyone?"

Olga shrugged. "There must have been trouble somewhere. Malfunction?"

"Hmm…Someone had better be here ASAP. This is crazy. There's…nobody here. I can't even hear people. It's creepy. We need our medical. I feel like falling over."

"Someone will be here," said Serj. "As you said, we need to get tested. I'm feeling a little light-headed. I need to take off the suit."

After a while, we all found a recovery room and got out of our suits. It took around an hour to get out of them, since usually we had more hands to aid in the transition. The suits were heavy and cumbersome, but once we were out of them, we all felt around fifteen kilos lighter. I felt as though I had shed a layer of skin, and breathed deeply, and enjoyed being liberated from the weight.

"God, I'm starving," I mumbled. "I just need to walk around, fill my stomach, then sleep. This mission took too long."

Olga looked at me pointedly.

"What? It's not like I caused the rocket failure."

"I didn't say anything."

"You didn't have to."

I shook my head and walked off down the corridor, slowly limping. I had expected the halls to be buzzing with noises, voices, exhilarated shouts, yet there was nothing to indicate anyone else was at the station at all. It was bizarre.

I found sleeping chambers and we all retired, collapsing on the beds as though we had run marathons in winter tracksuits during the summer. My skin felt flushed, but I didn't feel ill. I assumed I was simply dehydrated. Dehydration had been a major issue for me while in orbit. Because my bodily fluids hadn't been pulled down by gravity, they had collected around my chest and head, making space an uncomfortable, nauseous experience. Most of my time had been spent urinating, though I had cut down my fluid intake almost in half. I had assumed my body would adjust quickly on Earth, though of course I was wrong.

I closed my eyes, and concentrated on my breathing, slowly drifting into my thoughts.

3

When I awoke, it was late afternoon. Everything was silent. Except the silence was deafening; we had been used to sounds, signals, radio, constant conversation. This quiet was loud and unpleasant.

We wandered around the complex for hours, searching for food, evidence that other people were here. *Something!* But to no avail. Not one single person crossed our path. We ended up walking in circles, walked laps of the complex, calling out *cooee* for anyone who might hear us.

Olga began to pale, and soon had to sit down and rest. We walked over to the visitor centre, and it appeared abandoned. There were no engineers, no electronics technicians, no-one. We were alone. Thankfully, after almost six hours of searching, we found food in one of the storage cupboards. Serj, Olga, and I collapsed on the floor, stuffing our faces with whatever we could get our hands on. After so long of eating pureed and dry-freeze food, the packets of chips, jerky, and assortment of nuts were a godsend. Olga was the first to vomit, and we all followed suit, then continued to gorge ourselves until we could physically eat no more.

We watched the sun descend below the horizon, and the light blue turn to deep shades of red and orange. When I was ten, my father told me that sunsets occurred because the sun sat very low on the horizon. He said the molecules and particles were part of the atmosphere, all of which affected the way light was reflected and directed. When light rays scattered, my father said, colourful sunsets bloomed, and the wavelength of the light and the size of the particles would determine which colour and design would appear. I didn't understand him back them, but over time I figured it out for myself and longed to see a sunset from space. I longed to see the sun bloom.

We slept. By noon the following day, we came to the conclusion that for whatever reason, nobody was coming to find us, and we decided to leave. The basement car park was filled with cars, some with doors left ajar, others with dead batteries. Only a few were drivable. Serj got into the driver's seat of a jeep, and Olga got into the front. I cautiously sat in the back.

"You can't be serious about driving?" I asked.

Serj looked at me through the rear-view mirror. "I honestly have no idea what's happening. I'm going to drive and see how long it takes to find someone. I'm guessing there was a shutdown, and everyone was evacuated. Still, they could have sent us a signal, anything."

I jumped out of the car. "I don't even know why I got in. You can't drive! Neither of us can. Your balance must be off. You have to wait twenty-one days. We all do. You know that."

Olga rubbed her eyes. "Fuck. I just need to get somewhere so someone can fix my fucking eyes. Look around you! There's no-one here. Something's gone wrong, and we need to find out what. We can take turns driving. The second someone feels lethargic, we swap." She looked at both of us pointedly. "Got it?"

My stomach churned as I looked down at my feet. I was exhausted; driving was the last thing on my mind. Yet the butterflies in my stomach persisted. I got back into the car.

"Okay."

We drove for hours. The space station was a huge facility about twenty kilometres from Canberra, close to Paddy's River valley. As the only tracking station still in use within Australia, I had assumed it would be a hive of activity. Yet there was no traffic to or from the station, nor in Canberra, where we stopped for fuel. There were also no trees. In fact, the landscape appeared barren, blackened by fire, or something similar. *Field burning*, I think it would be called. The crops, the weeds, the seeds were all gone, survived by charred scraps of splintered wood. The remaining trees looked poisoned. Serj took the wheel, and the rest of us slept. When I awoke, I thought I was dreaming. I was surrounded by trees, yet they were charcoal-coloured, some appearing dark purple, with lavender splotches here and there, the leaves almost crimson.

"What on Earth...?" I rubbed my eyes tiredly and sat up in my seat.

Serj was pale with fear. "I don't know. There were no trees at all, and now they're everywhere! Look!" He jumped in his seat as he pointed ahead. I scrambled to get a closer look, as my stomach sank.

The land was black. It appeared barren, dead, the river a dark green sludge we were all too terrified to go near. The grass around it was dank and dead, and a horrendous swampy smell filled our nostrils, causing us to choke. Olga began to cry silently, and as I turned to see if she was alright, my jaw dropped in horror, for her eyes were bleeding.

"Stop the car!"

Serj skidded to a halt, and I climbed over the gearbox to the back seat, my hands on Olga's face. She blinked at me drowsily, her eyes unfocused, rivulets of blood and sweat running down her cheeks.

"What are you doing?" she sniffed.

I stared at her in horror. "Your eyes are bleeding!"

Her skin appeared jaundiced, her eyes bulbous and yellow. Her face was jaundiced, eyes bulbous and yellow. She rubbed at her skin softly, and small strips came away on her hands like seared meat. Screams rang in our ears; Serj attempted to wrap his arms around her, but Olga pushed him away, jumping out of the jeep and running out into the barren land.

At first, neither of us moved. We watched as she pulled and scratched at her skin, the lumpy flesh falling from her cheeks. Our bodies had frozen in fear. I couldn't go after her, even though I wanted to. Finally, she collapsed, and Serj went after her, screaming her name. I sat in the jeep, my hands and stomach in knots. My body was screaming for me to get out of the car and help Olga, yet my legs felt like stone. My body hunched over, and I began to comfortably rock, rubbing my hands across my eyes.

About twenty minutes later, Serj returned to the jeep. I looked up to see a pale-faced man stricken with shock. He slowly shook his head, his eyes wild and frantic.

"What do you mean, she's dead?" I hissed.

"She just…collapsed," he replied hoarsely. "Her skin is—what's left of it—it's covered in lesions. It's like she was infected by something, something in the air."

"That's impossible!" I exclaimed, frantically wringing my hands. "We're all breathing the same air." I jumped out of the jeep in shock.

"I don't know!" he shouted. "I don't know what's happening any more than you do!" He dropped to his haunches and rubbed his forehead. I came around the other side of the jeep and knelt down beside him, fingers in my mouth. I looked around us. For as far as I could see, the land was black. Everything was dark and dead and dangerous. I took a deep breath and closed my eyes. I had been through hours of safety training, grief counselling, psychological testing, but nothing had prepared me for this. This was an anomaly.

I looked behind me and narrowed my eyes, spotting something dark in the distance.

"What is that?"

Serj turned to peer at what I was looking at, shielding his vision with a hand on his brow. "Hmmm…"

We continued to watch it, until Serj jumped to his feet. "It's coming towards us!"

"What?" My stomach dropped as I realised he was right. It looked like some kind of vehicle, though it was moving too fast to be a car. Within moments it stopped in front of us, and we didn't have enough time to get a closer look before five official-looking people stepped out of the vehicle, spears pointed to our chests. Except they weren't people.

I gasped. Serj almost fainted. The five creatures looked amphibious; they were tall, and thin, with large black oval eyes, bald heads, with large gills instead of cheeks. Their skins were all different variations of aqua, some darker or lighter than others; one had yellow specs along its jaw line and yellow lips. Their noses were flat, except for a sharp mountainous ridge that sloped in the middle. All were fairly muscular, though two had clearly defined ribs that made them thin, but not unhealthy-looking. Most of them were naked, although I couldn't see anything that would resemble what I would believe to be a reproductive organ.

One of the creatures wore a string of pearls around its neck. It stepped forward and raised its arm.

"Who are you?"

Its voice was deep and masculine. As it talked, I noticed its thin lips dribbled what appeared to be something akin to saliva, except it was pale green and emitted a foul odour that smelled worse than the land around us. Their bodies were wet and slimy, and the smell was slowly becoming almost overbearing. I gagged. Serj vomited.

"Can you understand me?"

I nodded quickly. "Yes, I can understand you."

"Are you the leader of your flock?"

I frowned. "My…flock?"

The creature spoke tersely. "Yes, your flock. Are you the leader? Who is your leader?"

My mind was spinning, yet somehow, I managed to understand what the creature was saying. I panicked and pointed at Serj. "This is Serj Lindgren. He has the most experience." Serj looked at me as though I had blamed him for a murder he didn't commit. "But we're all equal," I added.

"Where are you from? Your skin is so dry and pale. Are you ill? You're all very ugly."

I wondered if I was hallucinating from the shock of being back on Earth. Or perhaps I was still in space. If I was hallucinating, then why did Serj seem just as surprised and terrified as me? Perhaps we had been exposed to something.

"We're human," Serj interjected, giving me a quick, icy glare. I hadn't realised my daydreaming had caused tension.

"Well, yes, of course you're human," the creature replied irritably. It appeared to consult with its friend, and then turned back to face us. "What continent are you from?"

"Australia, where we are now."

"Ostraya? Oh, we've gone too far. We were looking for Ant-Artikka."

"Antarctica?" I asked, my voice quivering.

"Yes, yes!" the creature replied. "We were told to meet at the base. Is it near here?"

Serj and I shook our heads in unison. "You're on the wrong continent. This is Australia. Antarctica is about... Oh gosh, what would it be? It takes around nine hours by plane," Serj said, his voice shaking. "Depending on where you leave from, of course. We're quite far away."

He was babbling. I stared at the creature in shock, surprised Serj and I were still conscious. Maybe the ship crash landed, and we were knocked out in a fiery wreck somewhere? Perhaps this was all a dream? That would make sense of the deserted space station.

"Os-Tray-Li-A? Oh! Our navigator put in the wrong coordination. Stupid! You led us to the wrong destination. We must be near one of the settlements."

"What settlement? What are you talking about?"

One of the other creatures stepped forward and gestured to Olga with its spear, swiftly flicking its tongue. "She is contaminated."

It came around to the jeep and pointed its spear at Olga's chest, elbow raised to press it through. I shouted and stood in front of her, barring its way.

"Don't hurt her!" I exclaimed wildly. "She's already dead, you savage! There must be something in the air, some toxin, that we are immune to, but she wasn't. Can you...can you tell me more about the settlement? Where is it?"

One of the creatures crossed its arms. "You must come with us. Flocks of humans are housed together in settlements until they are to be of use."

I looked at the creature, at its bulbous eyes, its wet skin, its inhuman expression. I had never been more terrified in my life. "Flocks of humans? But Earth is our home."

The creature narrowed its eyes and raised its spear threateningly.

"Not anymore."

4

Welcome to the Surface! The Surface is rich in minerals and plants, animals and grains, and an abundance of above-sea water which you must not, under any circumstance, touch or drink. Earth's water is toxic and there is no cure. Find your mate, find your place, and live in accordance to the law.

The creature drove for about half an hour, past several billboards and warning signs, finally stopping at large cluster of buildings surrounded by a crudely-made stone and iron fence in the middle of a patch of barren-looking land. It drove through a guarded gate and parked inside a moss-green shed, then roughly pulled us out of the jeep. Several creatures stared at us, some in intrigue or fear, as we were taken into a dilapidated building with brick walls and a corrugated iron roof. There were rows of long tables, filled with adults shovelling what looked like porridge into their mouths with a variety of utensils. A teenage girl cried as she attempted to eat with only three fingers.

Everybody was dressed in mismatched clothes, some wearing patterned headscarves, others wearing socks but no shoes. Serj and I were roughly pushed around and forced to sit at one of the tables. Olga was taken away down a corridor.

"Where are you taking her?" I demanded.

The creature ignored me and pushed a plate of grey porridge in front of me. "She is contaminated. Eat."

I stared at the slop, my stomach churning. As hungry as I was, I couldn't bring myself to eat the food. "Please, just tell us what's going on. Where are we, and where are you taking Olga?"

"Eat."

Serj clasped my wrist in terror, his hands clammy and cold on my skin. "Please, just tell us where you're taking her!" he pleaded.

"Eat! I won't ask you again."

The creature walked away before Serj and I could muster up an adequate response. Around us, everyone continued to eat their food, their heads bowed as if in meditation. The room was cold, and I shivered in the thin cotton shirt and pants I had worn under my spacesuit as we left the shuttle. We had all been in too much of a state of shock to think about changing our clothes.

After about half an hour of staring into my bowl of slop, a loud bell tolled in the distance, and I looked up to see where it had come from. A few people looked around in fear, others began to cry. Five of the creatures moved forward into the eating area and roughly grabbed a woman with a hemp sack over her entire body, dragging her to a small dais in the centre of the eating area. In the middle of the dais was what I'd assumed was a confusingly- placed flagpole, though it turned out to be some sort of torturous humiliation post. The woman was tied to it with thick ropes around her shoulders, waist, and ankles. Serj grabbed my wrist, and I was startled to feel his body shudder. I looked at him, and he looked at me, and we exchanged a similar feeling of intense fear.

"Silence! The retribution has begun!"

Serj and I whipped our heads to face the dais as one of the creatures, wearing what looked like a Native American headdress, stood forward to address the crowd.

"This creature has brought death and disease to us all! Her death was a blessing, though not before she contaminated us with her human ailment. Let this be a warning to the other humans who walk among us. We are not your guests; we are your liberators. We come in peace, but also in war. You humans have destroyed your land with fire and ash and black waste and we are here to transform it! We rose up from the ocean for one purpose and one purpose only: to curb your destructive appetite and prevent you from destroying Earth altogether!"

The creature pulled off the hemp sack, and my stomach churned in fear. Olga had been stripped to her undergarments, her skin red raw. I could see that she was shaking, her bottom lip quivering. Her eyes darted around the room, settling on no-one, until she found our faces; her eyes bulged in fear and she opened her mouth, yet she seemed incapable of uttering a single sound.

"Olga!" I shouted her name before I could think about my

actions, and jumped up from the table, running to the dais. One of the larger creatures stepped behind me, pulled a whip from its belt, and flicked it towards me. I felt it slice through the air and panicked, but it was too late, for the thin leather wrapped itself around my neck threefold, cutting into my jugular. The pressure built up in my throat instantaneously, and I rapidly felt light-headed, feeling the bloodflow leave my head. My hands dove for the leather whip, my nails digging into my skin. The world began to spin, to fade, and try as I might, I could not break free from the bond. I gasped once more, my tongue lolling, drool sliding down my chin. My eyes flickered as I looked over to see a spear flung straight through Olga's chest. I heard the harsh, guttural screams of Serj, and turned to watch one of the creatures strike him across the back of his head. Turning back to Olga, I watched helplessly as her head bowed, and her body fell limp. I heard the cracking of the whip, and I saw no more.

5

The barbeque smoke filled my nostrils, though I did not move from my place on the veranda step. I watched as my dad expertly turned over the sausages and tossed a handful of onions on the hotplate. He turned to me and smiled.

"Did you know that a day on Venus is longer than a year? Or that one million Earths can fit inside the sun?"

"Really, Dad?"

"Yep. And guess what's cool? Space isn't actually that far away. In theory, if you could drive your car upwards, you'd be in space than less than an hour!"

He handed me a small piece of sausage, and I laughed. "That's just silly. You're making that up. Space is so far away."

"Not really," he replied. "Hey, do you want to hear a joke?"

I looked up to the sound of the fly-screen door clattering and waved to mum and she came outside to have a cigarette.

"Did you hear about the cow astronaut? He landed on the moooooonnnnnn!!!!!!"

I awoke to the sounds of what seemed like childish laughter ringing in my ears. My stomach screamed in hunger, and I noisily vomited on the ground beside me. Looking around, I saw I was in a prison cell, my ankles shackled to the ground. On the wall across from me was a sign.

Welcome to your prison cell. You have not lived in accordance to the law and will incur punishment. Meals will be provided every eight hours. Do not try to escape or you will be exterminated immediately.

I attempted to jump up from the ground and winced, almost snapping both of my shackled ankles in the process. My eyes darted around the room, taking in my surroundings. The cell couldn't have been more than six by six feet and had a window even a child couldn't have escaped from. A thick iron door barred me from the outside, with a small slit down the bottom just big enough for a food tray. In the corner was a humiliating squat toilet, which judging by the stench, had not been cleaned for a while. Beside that was a pile of straw.

"Help!"

My throat burned as I croaked out the useless word. I didn't expect a saviour to come rushing to release me, but there was little else for me to do.

"Help! Let me out of here, you barbarians!"

My hands struggled at my metallic bonds, uselessly pulling, my shaking fingers dripping with sweat. I flung my hands against the walls over and over again in a stupid attempt to create a crack in the shackles, my shrill cries growing more hysterical by the second. I spluttered and coughed up dark maroon phlegm, spitting it on my vomit so they formed a putrid liquid mess. My throat and neck were in agonising pain, and my ribs were suffering a similar fate. I must have been kicked after I had passed out.

"What did I do to you all?! I'm an astronaut! I wanted to find you!" I shrieked. "We can learn from each other!"

"Did you ever think that maybe we didn't want to be found?" came a quiet voice from the other side of the door.

"Who is that? Who's there?"

I stared at the door and watched in horror as a thin, wet hand slid through the slot. I slid back into the corner of my cell, pressing myself against the wall.

"You smell different when you're awake."

"What?"

"I said you smell different when you're awake. You have lovely skin. I can't wait to wear it."

My heart felt like it dropped into my stomach, and I pressed my cheek against the wall, my eyes closed. "Please go away," I said, my voice barely above a whisper. "Just go away."

"But why? I want you to know what's going to happen to you. I've been watching you for a while now. I'm going to miss you when you're gone."

The voice was masculine, yet it was light, and almost youthful. I wondered how old the creature was, or whether the concept of age existed for them.

"I hope you don't scream as much as the last one. He howled like a hunted beast. It was almost too much."

Tears ran down my nose and slid over my lips. "Who?" I whispered. "Who screamed?"

"The one with the odd voice. With big brown eyes and messy brown hair."

"Oh no…no…"

Serj's face flashed before my eyes. His gentle smile, the crinkly lines around his eyes, his deep booming laugh.

"What did you do with him?" I asked. "Where is his body?"

"It's right here."

I whimpered as the bolt on the door was drawn, and it swung open, revealing a sight so horrendous I could have scratched my own eyes out to avoid the image appearing in my nightmares forevermore. Standing before me was Serj, yet it was only his skin that I stared at in horror, hanging loosely over that creature. His face, torso, and arms had been peeled completely from his body, and were crudely sewn on to the creature's own amphibious skin. The creature smiled, showing brown, jagged teeth jutting through Serj's purplish lips. Its expression was innocent and calm, and as I screamed, I was overcome by how absurdly human the creature must have been feeling. Was this its greatest ambition brought to life? Was this what the horde of controlling aliens wanted with us?

I couldn't tell how much time passed. I fell in and out of sleep, my dreams riddled with long corridors and faceless astronauts. When I awoke, the creature was still there, and there was nothing to do but continue screaming. My throat, already ablaze with pain, felt like razor blades were slowly dragging themselves across the underside of my skin. The room began to spin, and I vomited once more, this time projecting it onto the creature itself, covering its chest and arms. It appeared nonplussed by my reaction. Perhaps it was used to such a response when it revealed itself to other hysterical humans. The rattling of my chains reverberated around the room, mingling with my tears, snot, and screams, and I pulled at them with all my strength. But it was not enough.

"Give me back my friend!" I thundered, my voice sounding more like a banshee wail than my own. "Give him back to me!" I cried helplessly. "Give him back!"

The commotion appeared to have caused a disruption, for two other creatures appeared, one wearing a human face I couldn't recognise, the other one that I could.

"Olga!"

The creature seemed like a patchwork Frankenstein copy of my cosmonaut colleague. Olga had obviously been scalped, as it now wore her hair as proudly as a ceremonial headpiece. Olga's face had also been crudely attached to the creature, her mouth a little lopsided.

"What is...the point...of this madness?" I coughed, stumbling over my words. "Why? You...you said you didn't want to be found. So why are you here?"

"You humans and your explorations!" the creature wearing Olga's face spat. "You couldn't leave us alone, could you? Thousands upon thousands upon thousands of years we've existed and then you come along and destroy our home! Our habitat! You want to own everything. You're such selfish creatures. We're sick of you humans destroying our lives! You spill oil and poisons and toxins and leave sunken ships to rot in our backyards. Well not anymore! We're taking our lives back, and we're taking yours away!"

My body shook as I tried to process everything the creature

159

was saying. It didn't make any sense. Surely the world would have known about an amphibious species.

"But how do you survive?" I asked meekly. "How do you breathe? Where do you come from?"

One of the other creatures smiled. "Another planet, from another time. It was destroyed, and we sought solace in your oceans. It gave us time to study you. Your organs work wonders. You see, our bodies aren't that different after all. Slap in a pair of lungs, add an extra heart…construct a face out of human tissue… and there you go. We're human."

I stared at the hideous creature, at its bald, aqua head, the mountainous ridge on its nose, its dark black eyes. It looked like a creature that had failed its metamorphosis, a caterpillar not quite a butterfly, yet too small for its cocoon. It was ugly.

"You'll never be human!" I shouted, feeling my cheeks flush hotly. "Being human isn't about looking like one…it's about being humane!"

The creature appeared to laugh, snorting contemptuously. "But humans are not humane! You are all superficial hypocrites. You are all disturbed. You do not deserve your own planet."

"But *life* is disturbing! We are all disturbed. Perhaps because our lifespans are so incredibly short!" I replied hastily, my chin quivering in fear. "How can you claim to know us? Or how we feel? The world does not always spin the way you want it to, but that doesn't mean it's not spinning at all."

The creature wearing Serj's face tossed back its head and laughed. "You mourn your own species! Don't pretend to understand it. We've observed you and we know exactly what you think, how you feel. Humans just want to burn the world and everything in it."

"You must listen to me!" I exclaimed. "Humans are… We are more than physical beings. We seek knowledge, we are the keepers of knowledge. We study ourselves, our relations to other people, and in the end, to God. Yes, we're a paradox. We are the only species that straddles the divide between matter and spirit. We do not just inhabit the material world—we interpret it, discern order within it, derive meaning from it, and act decisively upon it. Our intellects transcend their material confines with a unique freedom and imagination. Can't you see that? You say you studied us, but you obviously missed the point. I feel sorry for you."

"Lovely speech," the other creature said, smirking. "But we are proof there is no God. We are proof your God is dead."

The two creatures lunged at me, and my limbs exploded in a panic, thrashing violently as one of them released my shackled ankles. They pulled at my arms as I attempted to roll out of their grasp, my torso oscillating wildly. The room turned dark as one of the creatures roughly pulled a hessian sack over my head, and my lungs began to wheeze in the stuffy entrapment.

I was thrown over the shoulder of one of the creatures and felt the excruciating slap of the whip on the back of my legs. I bit down on my tongue, hot tears running down my cheeks.

"Humans claim to have reason and intellect," one of the creatures boomed. "Yet we see no evidence of such. You constantly condemn your own kind: you cage them, starve them, debase them, dehumanise them. You are more barbarous than the species you slaughter for food. We can help you," he added angrily. "We can help you regain your compassion and benevolence. You don't have to be this way."

"What about the joy of just being alive?" I cried, as the whip continued to strike me. I was carried down a long corridor. Soon enough I heard voices, which quickly rose to conversing chatter. The hairs on my arms stood up, and goose bumps quickly inflamed my skin. I realised I had been taken to the dining hall. My heart thumped against my chest like it was motorised. It could only mean one thing.

"Why can't we just enjoy the efficacy of life?" I shouted, thrashing around on the creature's shoulder. "You don't have to understand it! Most of us never will anyway! Please, just let me go! This is foolish! This is wrong! You can't persecute me just because you don't understand me!"

"Be quiet, you loquacious fool!'

The whip struck me repeatedly, this time across the face, and my body fell into a bout of spasms as I tried to catch my breath. My skin felt like it was on fire, and I bit down on my lips, drawing blood.

As soon as we reached the hall, the creature dropped me to the ground, and I landed clumsily, my limbs stiff and aching from being bound for so long. One of the larger creatures picked me up from my waist and placed me on what I could only assume was the dais. My suspicions were confirmed as my body was tied to the flagpole. I was trembling, and my legs gave way, causing me to hang limply from the rope that had been secured around my stomach. I felt two long, slimy hands straighten my legs and tie them to the pole, wrapping the rope round and round my shins and thighs so if my muscles failed, I would not fall.

Then, there was silence.

THE PERFECT SON

The house seemed to have collapsed inwardly on itself, like a loaf of bread taken out of the oven too soon. The roof sagged, and the cedar shingles stuck up in places like wonky teeth. The lean-to shed on the side hung downwards as if the fight had left it and it could no longer bring itself to stand up against the elements. Yet Catherine couldn't leave. Her husband had begged her to sell the house, to move somewhere new. But memories tugged at her with thin, spidery hands, memories of happier times when the house was fresh and clean and filled with the laugher of a child.

She opened the refrigerator and stared at its contents. She hadn't been shopping. There was nothing but leftover Chinese and vegetables. Sighing, she closed the fridge and turned around.

There he was.

He looked impossibly real, like an ordinary seven-year-old boy. His thin, pale arms were folded across his chest, his knees drawn up to his chin. His eyes were shut, his lips parted. Jean's chin wobbled as her breath caught in her throat. He opened his eyes.

"Mummy."

Catherine tripped over herself as she backed into the corner of the room.

"Mummy?"

Catherine clenched her teeth and blinked ferociously as a torrent of tears fell down her face. She gasped as she fought for breath, her chest heaving in agony. How could she have been so stupid? What had possessed her to do such a thing? Ever since he'd arrived, the house smelled of damp fruit. Not quite rotten, but almost there. Yet still, she could not move away.

"Mummy? What are you doing?"

It sounded exactly like him.

"Mummy?"

She must have forgotten to lock the gate. They'd searched the house first, screaming out his name, Adam going through the closets where William liked to hide. Then Catherine had gone out the front, worried she might have left the front door unlocked. She had walked around the side of the house, to the backyard, and spotted him instantly, lying face down in the slightly green pool. A bluish-purplish stain marked his face, the upper part of his chest, his lower arms, hands, and his calves. It looked like deep bruising, stark against the greyness of his unblemished skin. Catherine had cradled him to her chest and screamed so loud she thought her lungs and eardrums would burst. When Adam found them, he took one look at his son and collapsed.

"Please, Mummy, I want a sandwich."

His bright blue eyes blinked at her innocently, and she ran her hands across her face in anguish.

"Will you put mustard on my sandwich?"

Catherine tiptoed into the kitchen. He stared at her as she buttered the bread, her hands shaking. She unscrewed the lid from the mustard jar. He stood beside her and put his small hand on her arm.

"Mummy?"

Catherine stared out the window. They'd built the house on acreage, and while once she had loved the land, now it felt like a prison. Jean watched the blue fade to yellow, the horizon slowly sinking under the tops of the tall clustering of trees, the pastel colours of the gradually darkening sky. Along the hills, the trees obscured the sunset, dotting the skyline so suddenly it looked as though someone had plucked them from a forest and placed them where they stood for no other reason but to look at as they passed. Jean had loved to stare at the trees. Now all she saw was an expanse of grey—the greenery turned to ashes.

"Mummy! Look at me!"

Catherine jumped. The jar shattered on the ground, glass shooting across the linoleum. The boy brushed the light brown bangs from out of his face and grinned, showing small, pointed teeth.

"Clean it up, Mummy."

Catherine looked away from the window, shaking as she stared at the young boy pointing at the mess. She nodded and went to fetch the broom and dustpan, rushing back as fast as she could, and began to sweep. She watched as the boy effortlessly extracted a long slither of glass from his hand and bent to place it in the dustpan.

"Clean faster. I might hurt myself."

Catherine swept the broom faster. She wondered what would happen if she led the boy into the forest and left him there. When she had finished, she sprayed disinfectant on the floor and wiped it over with a paper towel.

"Good job, Mummy," the boy said. "I'm tired now. I need to sleep. Keep that sandwich for when I wake up. And set aside some clothes for me."

He stepped around Catherine and walked upstairs. Catherine stared at the mess in the dustpan, her hands shaking so much the little pieces of glass entwined with dirt and dust seemed to dance upon the blue plastic. She dropped the dustpan on the floor and ran out the front door, her legs thundering down the street.

Catherine came to rest in a small paddock, where her neighbours had constructed a park. The land around her was speckled with sheep. She cleared her throat as she stared at the greenery, at the mountains sloping towards each other, meeting at a deep crest in the middle. How could something that had once seemed so beautiful now feel like a barren wasteland? She collapsed into a swing and clenched the metal chains tightly, her knuckles whitening. Why didn't her husband see what she saw?

Why had she wanted another child? She could have given birth naturally, could have tried again with her husband. She could even have tried surrogacy. *But no.* The idea of having a son created just for her had been morbidly alluring. Her very own son; just like the one she had lost. In this way, her lost child could grow up the way he was supposed to, before his cruel, untimely death.

"Why did you leave me, Mummy?"

Catherine turned to find the boy sitting on the swing beside her, his little legs dangling in the air. He wore her lilac dressing gown, and it dragged behind his heels. In his hand was the underside of the mustard jar, broken and jagged around the edges.

"Well?"

Catherine bit down on her bottom lip. She pressed her hand to her forehead, feeling the coldness of her clammy skin.

"I didn't leave you. I promise I didn't. I just went for a walk."

The boy cocked his head, his limp brown hair falling across his face. He peered at her with one dark, beady eye. "I think you left me on purpose. I had to dress myself."

Catherine shook her head, her hands wrapped around the metal links of the swing so hard they began to hurt. She inhaled deeply, throat pained by the sharp coldness of the steadily growing wind, inclined to go back home, yet terrified to leave the park. She knew he would follow her.

"No, no, no I didn't, I promise, I would never hurt you. It was an accident, a mistake."

"You're good at arranging accidents, aren't you, *Mother*?"

Catherine bit down on her lip, tears running down her nose. "Please, I would never hurt you. Never."

"I don't know about that." The boy kicked off from the ground and began to swing. He leaned back so that his head almost touched the bark mulch and wood chips beneath them.

"You told Daddy it was his fault and that he was careless and left the gate open. You told him he was a monster and that it was his fault I was dead."

He swung higher.

"How do you know that?"

The boy smiled. "I wonder if you wanted a child at all."

"How do you know that?" she repeated anxiously.

He swung higher.

Catherine leapt off the swing and ran back to the dilapidated house. She bent over, gulped deep breaths, and staggered into the kitchen, turning to retrieve the jagged piece of glass from the mustard jar. Sweat swam down her neck. She collapsed on the floor against the fridge, sobbing.

"Are you making me that sandwich?"

Catherine leapt to her feet and brandished the glass in front of her. The boy stood in front of her, his arms at his side, his face pale, his eyes accusatory, ominous in the ridiculous, oversized dressing gown.

"Why bother bringing me back if you don't want me?"

Catherine sobbed, her hand covering her face. "But I do, I do want you, my baby. I do want you. I didn't know...I didn't know... You look..."

"What didn't you know? How should I look? Like the last time you saw me?"

Catherine peered through her fingers and stared at the boy, yet all she could see was her poor dead son, so pale and blue.

"Why are you doing this to me!?" Catherine screeched. She reached out and clasped the boy's hand, shaking it wildly. "Why? What do you want from me?"

The boy ran his thin, cold fingers through her hair and stared down at her, unsmiling. "The question is—what do *you* want from *me*? You were the one who spent your life savings to have me created. Does he know how you lied, you stole, how you cheated to get that money to pay for me? What were you planning to do? Dress me up for school, brush my hair in the morning, and pack me a lunch? I'm not your son, Catherine. You can't force me into your home."

He gently massaged her hair. Catherine brought the glass down swiftly, plunging it into the boy's neck.

"Mummy, why won't you play with me?"

Screaming, she turned and ran, and the boy chased after her, leaping to wrap himself around her legs so that she fell over, tripping on the rug in the hallway. The boy straddled her, the shard of glass protruding from his neck. He pulled it out slowly, showing no signs of agony.

"Get off me!" Catherine screamed.

She rolled over and pushed him off. He slammed into the wall and growled, leaping to his feet. He slashed the glass in front of him. Jean held her hands out in front of her and stared once more into the eyes of her son, her beloved son—knowing they were not really his —falling to her knees in a crumpled, defeated heap.

The boy stabbed the glass fragment down into her shoulder and through her chest, and she collapsed on to her back, her mouth opening and closing like a fish. He stood over her, face serene.

"Why?"

Catherine shook her head, exhausted.

"I'm sorry, I'm sorry, I'm sorry."

The boy shook his head sadly, his eyes downcast. "No. Why would you spend your life savings on a replicate of your deceased son? It makes no sense, Catherine. Is this your way of denying the existence of God?"

Catherine sat up, brushing away her tears. "What?"

"God," said the boy. He ran his fingers over his face, his nails digging into the soft flesh. "You know, that omnipotent being who creates human life?"

Catherine drew in a deep breath of air. "William?"

"Of course, I'm not William," the boy said. "I am simply a synthetic body you instructed to be programmed with your deceased son's characteristics. You gave a scientific organisation everything you are worth to have your son returned to you, without thinking of the consequences. Why can't you let him go?"

Catherine stared at the boy—who looked so much like her son—and searched for inconsistencies. He had William's mole, the little half-moon scar on his cheek, the almost unnoticeable bend in his arm where he had fallen from a tree the year before he died.

She stumbled to her feet, her hand on her bleeding shoulder.

"Just go away!"

The boy shook his head. "You have to deactivate my neural

processor. I am alive because you made it so—you are free to do as you wish."

Catherine glanced down at the shard of glass in her shoulder. The boy stared at her as if waiting for instructions, and she glanced around the room, looking for something that would amuse him.

"Do you want me to get out a puzzle?" she asked the boy.

He nodded. "Yes. Go and get it for me."

"Wait here."

Catherine left the boy in the kitchen and ran to the hallway. She pulled down the attic ladder and scrambled up, folding it up behind her and dropping to her knees. Her chest throbbed in agony, and she began to wheeze, feeling light-headed. What had she done? There was something so wrong about the boy masquerading as her son. She looked around the cramped space—it was hardly an attic—and stared out of the tiny window that overlooked the road below. She could see her neighbours arriving home from work, the woman down the street with her dog, and a few kids riding past on their pushbikes.

Maybe she could lull the boy into a false sense of security, read him a bedtime story, stroke his head until he fell asleep— did he sleep? —and then slit his throat. *But he wasn't human!* She looked at the glass in her shoulder and attempted to pull it out, gasping in pain. Breathing deeply, she closed her eyes and held the shard tighter, blood spilling from her hand as she wrangled with it, feeling it extract itself inch by inch as she pulled. She let out a strangled cry as she pulled it from her shoulder.

"Mummy, what was that noise?"

Blinking back tears, Catherine wiped the underside of her hand across her face. "Nothing, dear. Just wait there. I'm looking for the puzzle. It's...messy in here."

She had to get out of the house. She looked at her watch and gasped. Adam would be home soon.

"Mummy! The puzzle!"

Catherine closed her eyes and thought back to the day she had signed the waiver and consent form. The woman had plucked a shiny new pen from the bun in her hair and had handed it to her with such a genuine smile that Jean couldn't say no.

"You understand this is only temporary?" the woman said.

Catherine nodded. "Of course. I won't get attached."

The woman smiled. "It's best if you do everything you normally would do to give yourself time to adjust. After the trial period, you can let us know if you'd like to acquire the subject permanently."

"Oh, but I've already made up my mind. I mean, my husband doesn't know just yet, but he will be so happy. I don't need time to think. I know I will love him just as much as I loved William. He's my second chance."

"Yes," said the woman, "only you must realise the subject will have the capacity to make its own choices, form its own opinions. You need to consider the possibility that it may not love you. At least, not at first. The subject needs time."

Catherine closed her eyes and took a deep breath. "I understand. But that's a risk I am willing to take. It's been two years, and I still wake with the same sadness I had the day Anthony died," Catherine murmured. "People say, 'I want the old Catherine back,' but they don't know the horror I witnessed in that morgue, in that tiny coffin. It's not humanly possible for me to be the person I was. I would be a monster."

"Mummy, where is the puzzle?"

Catherine looked out the window. She dropped the shard of glass and scrambled over to it, turning the lever and pulling it open. She sucked in a breath and began to climb through it, head reeling as she stared at the ground below her. She'd chosen the two-storey house for its location; near a school, a park. But now, as she stared down at the grass, she realised she had made a mistake. If she landed at a bad angle she could break her leg, or worse. And he would get her.

Catherine heard the boy climbing the stairs, and she pushed her body through further so that her head and torso were outside. Across the road, one of her neighbours was tending to his garden, and he looked up at her, shading his eyes with his hand.

"Hey! Hey you! I need help!"

The man cocked his eyebrow and stared at her in horror.

"Hey! Dave. Dave! Please help me!"

She looked down at the ground as she attempted to get her

knee through the small window. Grunting, she tried to push it through, but it was stuck. Sweat dribbled down her face and spilt over her lips, and she cried as she pulled her leg back in the window. She would have to go feet first.

Knock, knock, knock.

"Go away!"

"But you're supposed to love me. Aren't I the perfect son? What did you expect of a replacement child? Did you sit in the waiting room, your and my father, your defeated bodies like husks waiting for the process to be over so you could both wither and die? What happened after your son died? Did they send cards on his birthday, at first? Did the cards stop coming? Anthony, the child. Anthony, the dead child. Anthony, the dead child in the coffin."

Catherine pressed her hands over her eyes, jaw clenched. "Stop it! Just shut up! Go away!"

The boy kicked open the door, and he stared at her with his dark, emotionless eyes. "You killed me. You're supposed to love me. I'm a poor, defenceless child."

"You're not my fucking child! I didn't give birth to you!"

Catherine looked down at the ground below, then back to the boy. His face began to twitch, as though he were struggling with which emotion to display. What the hell was he?

She leapt away from the window and lunged at him, her nails digging under the skin along his jaw. The flap of skin pulled back easily, revealing a mechanical face, flashing red eyes, with twisted tubes pumping black liquid up through his nose and mouth. She screamed and stumbled backwards, and the boy smiled.

"We're the same, you and I, Mummy. Cold and metallic on the inside." He grabbed Jean's hand and slapped it against his chest.

"What are you?" she whispered, sweat and tears dripping down her nose.

"I'm your son."

As he spoke, he began to peel back the rest of his synthetic face, until his entire mechanical head was revealed, his fleshy face hanging on the back of his neck like the hood of a jumper.

"Do you think you're God?"

Catherine shook her head. "Of course not. I was just lonely. I needed you."

The boy smiled, his metallic mouth a twisted line. "I think you took the power of God in your own hands and warped it to suit your own selfish desires. I am but a prototype, and you neglected to think of the outcome of your little experimentation. I'm a burden to you. But I'm not lonely. I don't need you like you need me. You already killed one child. Why bother with another?"

Catherine lunged at the boy angrily and picked him up. The boy kneed her in the face, knocking her sideways, so her shoulder hit the wall. Swiftly, he pulled at her arm, dislocating it, and kicked her knees. She dropped to the ground in pain. He grabbed her arms with incredible strength and dragged her over to the window, pushing her torso out so that she could see Adam pulling into the driveway. She turned to face the boy, and he smiled, pushing her out of the window. She fell face-first onto the windscreen of Adam's car, legs akimbo, pale against the dark matte of the car.

The boy raised his hand, smiling.

"Hello, Daddy. It looks like it's just you and me now."

THORNE HOUSE

Siouxsie hadn't expected they'd get lost so easily. The roads seemed to twist considerably more than the map suggested, deviating from their planned route so drastically Budge had all but given up. Their begrudging quiet seemed preferable to their bickering, yet neither wanted to admit defeat. Instead, they sat in stony silence, save the occasional huff. While the morning weather had suggested it wouldn't be dark for hours, already the skies blazed a lurid purple, intermingled with blotches of yellows and oranges, signalling twilight. Siouxsie wound up the window firmly, curling towards the passenger door. Ahead, the sign for the turnoff seemed overtaken by plants, and she gestured to it soundlessly, sleepily rubbing her eyes. They would soon reach the old guesthouse.

Budge turned on the hazard lights and steered the car towards the turnoff, driving down the narrow dirt road, eyes gazing the field ahead for signs of life. The road seemed to stretch endlessly, the railings curving left as the hill grew steeper and the car climbed up the mountainside. The road became narrow, the thorn bushes creeping closer to the car until Siouxsie felt almost swallowed by the great thorny beast, the vines and prickles scraping over the windscreen of the car like long, sharpened fingernails. Above, the sky melted into a dark velvety lilac, the yellows fading just above the stone roof of the decrepit guesthouse.

Siouxsie followed Budge out of the car, clinging to her husband's shirt sleeve as she struggled to make out shadowy movements in the window of the house. Budge rolled his eyes and pressed on. Siouxsie ambled along beside him wordlessly, eyes darting around the darkness in suspicion.

The greenish brass knocker looked heavy, yet Budge picked it up with ease, dropping it with a loud bang. The pair waited silently on the doorstep. Siouxsie shivered as a single raindrop fell from the sky and rolled down the back of her neck. She brushed it away and stumbled forwards. Budge shrugged, taking her movement as a cue to enter, and roughly pushed open the door. Siouxsie gasped. Down the hallway, in the parlour, overhanging a large ornate fireplace, hung a large portrait of a man surveying the very house in which they stood. He held a pipe in one hand and pointed towards the house with the other. Although the man's robust features and fine clothing suggested class and wealth, his face wore a dismal frown, his blue eyes wide and foreboding. He seemed to be looking at something with intense fear.

Siouxsie tugged at Budge's sleeve once more, and they pressed on, moving from room to room in search of signs of life. They turned down a narrow hallway covered in floral wallpaper, yellow flowers strangled by twisted purple vines. Siouxsie wiped the beads of sweat from her neck. Ahead, a meagre light flicked on, illuminating the hallway. Siouxsie clasped Budge's hand and pulled him forwards, determined to find the proprietor. The light flickered off. It flickered on. The couple jumped as they stared at the portrait in disbelief, now cemented on the wall at the end of the hallway. Siouxsie stood still, neck elongating to peer at the end of the hall.

Budge motioned towards the end of the corridor, and they made their way further into the house. Budge pulled Siouxsie through an open door. Siouxsie gasped at the sight of many framed portraits and mirrors hanging on what looked like sloping walls. The roof of the room formed a steeple above them, enclosing them in the small, stuffy space. Siouxsie felt the prickle of fingers on her neck and spun around, eyes wide at the sight of the purple vines twisting across the doorway, barring their escape.

Thorns crept down from the walls, slithering around her body, enclosing her in the flowery cocoon. The portrait rattled on the wall. The man's face shifted to reveal a reflection identical to Budge's. Its mouth curled in a twisted smile. The thorns squeezed tighter. Siouxsie screamed.

DEEP-SEA FISHING

The rain was torrential, scudding against the sloped roof of the boat. I stowed my belongings under the deck, shakily signing my name on the boat's manifest. Thomas handed me a piece of paper with my bag number.

"Alright there, son?" Dad called from on board. "Get in, get in, away from the storm."

I nodded, looking up at the wraithlike shadows accumulating in the sky. "I'm good."

"Did you catch the safety equipment talk?"

"Yep."

Dad nodded. "Don't mind the weather. A storm never frightens the fish away."

Pete spoke over the intercom about the safety equipment, how to rig up, and gave an overall rundown of the night ahead. Dad told me there was an allure to deep-sea fishing which had nothing to do with the fabricated excitement of TV shows.

"It's more relaxing than you think," he said. "We don't wrestle with giants. We think about them."

It took thirty minutes to get out into the fishing grounds, the rain bucketing for most of the duration. Pete set up the rental gear and passed out raincoats, giving us all a quick 101. While most of the guys stuck to their beers; I kept my ears open, eyes sharp.

"Be careful you don't fall in," said Dad.

"Don't want to be sleeping with the fishes," Aaron joked. He pulled the binoculars away from his watery blue eyes. He appeared more interested in birds than humans and noted the different types he spotted in his notebook. Before we left that afternoon, Aaron had said we'd cross paths with bird migrations unperturbed by the storm, swooping around the pitch-black curtains draped across the sky like warped, twisted shapes ducking in and out. However, the creatures above were lost and confused, some dropping from the sky altogether to land on the patches of driftwood floating by the boat.

"What are they doing?" I asked, hooking my bait. "Should we tell someone? The marine people? Why are they out so late? I thought they weren't bothered by the weather."

"The *marine* people?" Dad joked.

Aaron shrugged. "Not sure, lad. Best to leave them to their devices."

I nodded. I'd watched Dad with Aaron for years. His face had carved up a perpetual expression for Aaron, one mixed with both pride and pity. I hated them both.

I spent the next few hours on deck until the sun sank, and we waited for midnight. Rain fell intermittently, though not hard enough for us to head below deck. I stood by the railing, line in both wet hands, staring at the mass of dark water. Time slowed as my fingers fiddled with the squid, waiting patiently for the greenlight to drop hook. Once the boat settled, I dropped my first line.

The fish came in like a pack of wild dogs, snarling, sniffing, clawing their way into the boat. I pulled my shirt over my nose, trying not to breathe in the rotten scent. Dad and Aaron pulled in the first batch, opening the hatch, pulling out the tarpaulin, until the fish were tucked away under the deck.

"You gonna help me, son?" asked Dad, "I'm doing the work of two men." Aaron glanced at me, face impassive. I sighed, disheartened my hook had failed to catch anything.

"I'm going down for a sec," I said, attaching my rod to the side of the boat. Dad waved his hand in acknowledgement.

Above, I could hear the laughter of the men, their casual

conversation. I sighed, wishing I had the same euphoria the others felt out on the sea, though I suppose their passion had more to do with endurance in the dark storm than anything else. I was certain the love of deep-sea fishing was either a learned practice, or a coping mechanism by someone who felt rejected from society.

I walked down the dark, narrow hallway, peering out the little manholes at the smooth, unchanging water. Thoughts drifting, I pushed open the door of the room Dad and I shared. It was small and cramped, what one might expect in a deep-sea fishing boat. Most of the confined cupboards contained fishing gear, raincoats, and endless packets of biscuits. The walls were panelled in wallpaper meant to resemble wood, the floors covered in rolls of crudely cut linoleum. To the left were a small enclosed shower and toilet, a stack of toilet rolls pushed in the corner, to the right a tall closet and corner lounge. I closed the door behind me and pulled off my raincoat, climbing the stepladder to lay on the bunk. I rolled onto my side and stared at the ornamental mirror on the wall.

"Ten thousand," Aaron said, his shadowy form appearing in my doorway. I jumped, sitting up.

"How did you get in here?"

"It's from the Elizabethan period. It's fine craftsmanship, a collector's item. Some fishermen say it exaggerates things, reflects yourself holding a great big Marlin, winning first prize. Others say it shows them something else."

I jumped off the bed, snorting contemptuously. "Like what? Their reflection?"

Aaron raised his brows, smirking. "You don't believe me. Your old man saw something in the mirror. Said a black smudge appeared over his left eye while he was combing his hair. Next day, fishing hook catches his eyelid, ripping it from his face."

"Whatever. That's not how he got that scar."

Aaron shrugged. "Fine, don't believe me. But you should know Stuart was in this room before you, back when we were out for a whole month. He got a look at that mirror. He was your age. I told him about the mirror, your Dad's fascination with it, and I assumed it'd hold some curiosity for the boy. Maybe he'd appreciate its appearance in such a dingy old boat. But he didn't."

Crossing my arms, I traced the mirror's frame with my tired eyes. I couldn't deny the shiver of uneasiness I felt clasp the back of my neck like the talons of a slippery, ethereal beast. "It's an old mirror. No big deal."

"No big deal, huh? It's sure a big deal for your dad. And it was for Stuart. Until he hung himself." He shrugged noncommittally. "Your dad suggested we take you out to catch fish, spend a whole month together. But I said no, you wouldn't be up to spending so much time with us, with all that fish hanging on the boat for weeks. We say the fish is fresh, but can flesh stay fresh after hanging for so long? Can anything stay fresh after hanging for so long?"

Swallowing a lump of saliva, I watched as Aaron looked around the room with smug disinterest. The room itself was inexplicably hot, the mirror placed in such a way the moonlight beamed though the circular window, and a pearly light stretched across the wall behind the bunk.

"You gonna leave your line out?" Aaron said, stepping backwards. "Your dad paid good money for you to be here. Yet you hide from the storm."

"I'm not hiding," I snarled, wondering how anyone could think the storm was merely rain. Aaron rolled his eyes. I wanted to be interested in fishing, be interested in sticking it out during the long nights of darkness when the ocean grew quiet, and bankside vibrations and crisscrossing lines disappeared. I wanted to wait for the water to spring to life, as fish that refused to eat during the day let their guard down. But it all felt so menial in the storm.

"Lucien, we've got everything set up. It's piss-weak easy. Come on. Plenty of fish and flesh in the sea. You're supposed to embrace the storm."

I groaned, rubbing my eyes, imagining the rows of fish corpses waiting to be eaten. "Piss off!"

Aaron narrowed his eyes. "Come now," he said jovially, "I'm ya mate. Head up and see the clusters of bubbles, the disturbed silty patches, the topping fish. Use those words when you talk to your Dad. He might think you care."

"I do care! Piss off," I repeated, moving to stand by the mirror. "I'll be up soon."

"If you say so. Bring your raincoat."

Aaron winked, slinking into the darkness. Huffing, I peered into the mirror and stared at my reflection. Not for the first time, I wondered what such a thing was doing in the dingy quarters of a fishing boat. Who in their right mind would drag the mirror on board? I imagined a fish hook catching itself in my eyelid, and for a moment, it reflected in the mirror itself. I pressed my hands over my face, over my eyes, feeling for the hook. But there was nothing. Sighing, I moved to lean against the doorframe, chest heaving, fists clenched.

"Fucking arsehole."

On deck, Thomas fumbled with the digital scales, patting down his pockets. Pete stood on the side of the boat, line in. He seemed fixated on the water, eyes firm, the only man somehow not drenched. Dad sat on an overturned milk crate, soft rain pouring over his face. He pulled out a small pack of batteries from his tackle box, handing them to Thomas. I watched as they worked together to get the scales operational, smiling as Dad guffawed over the weight of the fish. A small, fat rat scrambled across the box, and Dad jumped, dropping the fish.

"Goddamned rats! C'mere, son. Hold this!"

Aaron appeared from below deck, nudging Tom. Tom stepped in front of me to catch the fish. I ducked in front of him as Dad gave me a swift pat on the back meant for Aaron. He leapt from the crate, eyes darting around for the fish. They were comfortable together, as though the only shelter they needed from the rain was each other. A crackle of thunder shot across the sky. However, none moved to go below deck, more interested in the guts of their fish, and the bloodied bottles of beer in their hands.

"Leave it, mate," Aaron said, picking his line from the side of the boat. He stood at the railing, facing the sea. Dad turned his attention to the scales.

"Horrible critters," Pete remarked, glancing over his shoulder. I looked over at him, at his straight back, content standing on the other side of the boat in the dark, in the pounding rain, waiting for fish. He caught my eye, and I moved to stand beside him.

"Hold this," he said, passing me the rod. I took it firmly in my hands, momentarily startled by the water's gentle hold, even in the stormy, forceful night. Pete crossed his arms, eyes scanning the darkness.

"Don't bother yourself with your dad," he muttered. "Thinks he knows a thing or two about everything."

"And the mirror?"

Pete's shoulders stiffened, eyes narrowing. "Leave it alone. You know, I looked at it, once. The room moved, if only by a few centimetres. The walls turned into odd angles, balancing so precariously it seemed they would slide away into the cracks in the floorboards."

I raised a dubious brow.

"I'm serious," Pete said. "A dark streak of something, smelling of tar, blackened the side of it, across my wrist. The next day while gutting a fish, I tripped over a bucket and sliced open my arm. Your dad saved me. It was a miracle I didn't bleed to death." He sighed, running a hand over his wet forehead. "But you want to know what was weird? The fish could smell my blood. Never had a better haul."

Shuddering, I gripped the rod tighter, eyes narrowed as I stared at the raindrops on the water. I wondered how anyone could see the fish. My hands felt unsteady, weak, and as I scanned the surface of the water for bubbles or any inclination of movement, I pondered whether Pete was telling the truth. He didn't seem the type to lie. Then again, most of the men on board were reserved. There was no telling what they thought. Or planned. Still, I knew Pete believed what he was saying to be true.

After another two hours of disconcerting disappointment, I realised my future would not be in the deep-sea fishing business and promptly gave up. I gazed across the cold, frothy ocean, at the low-hanging clouds, the reflection from the moon on the wavering water, imagining I was anywhere but here. Anywhere besides the middle of the ocean, with nothing but long stretches of water as far as the eye could see. Dismally, I pulled in my line and stored it away, heart falling. After a full eight hours of idleness and unfulfillment, I felt like a fraud. I felt Dad's gaze on me as I retired once more downstairs, sodden. I dared not look back, as I knew his eyes would reflect the same disenchantment and antipathy I had for myself. I had never liked thunder, nor storms. I wanted to forget I was ever part of the crew. I knew Dad had invited me to make use of my wasted night hours, but I returned below, dripping wet shoulders slumped in realisation Aaron had been right all along. I was seeking shelter; I was hiding. But not from the storm.

Wrapping a warm blanket around my shoulders, I sat on my bed, staring at the mirror. Rain trickled down the small, circular window, like icy, wet fingers, trying to claw their way in. I leant against the wall, my wet hair plastered to my forehead, wondering how the others managed to stay outside in the storm. It was getting early now, 4am, yet the storm did not abate. *Don't storms usually last around half an hour?* I wondered.

The illumination from the moonlight proffered indeterminate shadows on the walls, each one stretching longer than the last. The scent of fish encased the room, pressing itself upon the bed, on myself. I watched as the shadows crawled onto the ornate mirror, as if moving by their volition. Staring at my reflection, at the contorted angles of my cheeks, I wondered for the umpteenth time where the hell the mirror had come from. I didn't believe in ghosts, in monsters, in anything supernatural, but with mirrors... I wondered if there was more to see than my reflection.

As if detecting my curiosity, the mirror rippled. I stared at my reflection, at my sunken eyes, puffy cheeks, sallow skin, heart racing as I realised my unkempt appearance was as frightening as it was confronting. Six and a half hours on board an old fishing boat, and I had somehow become a shrunken, shrivelled, sodden version of myself. But it was not a sign I was unused to seeing. Insomniacs all looked the same. I checked my bulky waterproof watch, rolling my eyes at the lateness of the hour. It would be dawn soon, and I had not caught a single fish. *You haven't even tried,* I thought dismally. *Why are you hiding? Get back out there.* I stared out the window, bewildered by the continuing storm. I was no meteorologist, yet it seemed absurd the clouds had any more rain to give. Outside, the rain streaked across the glass like razors across an exposed throat. The boat rocked precariously against the gale, and the waves rose as great angry mountains, the choppy waters morphing into a landscape of its very own, wind slamming small pebbles, the waves' salt rising over the deck, angry, tumultuous, thirsty.

"Hey Lucien," I said to myself, staring at my reflection in the mirror, "when are you ever going to grow up?" The reflection was silent and still, save for my mute mouth, opening and closing like a suffocating fish. My skin was yellowed and tired, my face all forehead and no cheeks. I couldn't think of any successful fisherman with a face such as mine.

"I don't look like them," I muttered. "I can never be one of them."

"That's right."

I jumped, tripping over myself as Aaron strode into the room. His presence filled the entire room, robustly inserting itself into every nook and cranny.

"You're such a pansy," he said, pacing the tiny room, clothes dripping. "Almost ten thousand, it cost."

"You told me before."

Aaron nodded, pressing his wet hand against his mouth. "What are you doing here, skulking around?"

I frowned. "It's my room. I can skulk around it if I wish. Now, go away."

"Ah!" Aaron replied, "but it was my room first."

"So?"

"So, I can skulk around it if I want." He stared at me quizzically, then at the mirror, as if musing upon some great philosophical thought only he could solve. For a moment, he seemed interesting, and not the barbarous bully I knew him to be. *What does my dad see in you? Why on Earth does he keep you around? You're an intimidating thug. A low-life. And I hate you.*

"If you stay down here long enough looking at it, you'll go blind. Don't know why Pete bought it. It's a hideous piece of garbage."

My thoughts became a jungle of confusion. A trickle of sweat, mingled with water, ran down the back of my neck. "You said you paid ten thousand for it. Why would it be useless?"

Aaron narrowed his eyes, bemused. He ran a thick hand through his hair, sighing dramatically.

"I never said I paid for it, you snoop," he said, moving to lean against the wall. "I would never buy such a crappy old thing. Look at it. It's crap. A piece of junk. Why would I own it?"

I balled my hands in frustration, my heart thudding against my chest. I took a deep breath, inhaling the stale air, and let it out, eyes fixated on Aaron.

"Was there something you wanted?"

Aaron shrugged. "Thunderstorms, rain... Do you ever think they're supposed to wash us away?" he asked. "Are they supposed to drench us so we become nothing but a smudge in a Monet masterpiece?"

I shrugged, body rigid, an animal ready to attack, though I was still unsure of why I was afraid of the man.

"Rain can be different," Aaron continued. "Summer thunderstorms, droplets bouncing off cars in a quick burst of rain, torrential downpours. There are different types. Yet the fish don't seem affected by it." He moved around the room, stopping to glance at my duffel bag, at my shoes, my phone on the table beside the bunk. I bit on my tongue.

"You know, fish are sensitive when it comes to the weather. They sense changes in water pressure. Insects flitter when it's sprinkling, buzzing around, enticing the fish to the surface. Rain makes humans head indoors, seek shelter with one another, but not here, out in the ocean. Not fish. When it rains, the fish come out to play. And the humans are ready."

I ran my tongue along my bottom row of teeth, hastily burying my hands in my pockets. A shiver ran down my back. "What are you saying?"

Aaron shrugged, feigning disinterest. "Oh, nothing," he replied, moving over to the door. "It's…" He paused, shrugging. "Never mind."

"What?"

"Well… There's a story about the mirror. You sure you haven't heard it?"

I shook my head irritably. "No."

Aaron nodded, pouting his bottom lip. "The story goes a fisherman once owned the mirror. Years back, hundreds of years back. He was the only survivor on a ship that sunk. He washed up on shore, somewhere on one of the Moreton Bay islands. When the other bodies were found, it seemed there'd been an attack on the boat—knife wounds, gunshot wounds, even decapitation. You name it, those bodies had it. One man even had his eyes missing. But nobody knows who the fishermen were, since all their names, all their families, disappeared."

I pulled my hands from my pockets and wrapped my arms around my waist, nodding. "Go on."

"Your dad told us they were taken by pirates, marauders, anyone looking to make money. Back then, all the land was farmhouses, cousins marrying cousins, one pub between three towns… You get the idea."

Aaron curled his upper lip, looking over at the window, gazing out into the inky black night. "Anyway, the boat washed up around the Cleveland Point lighthouse, the original one built in 1847. You know how the second lighthouse, the one now standing, is hexagonal rather than round?"

I nodded, moving to sit on the edge of the bottom bunk. I curled my fingers under the mattress, the palms of my hands coated in sweat.

"This is because of what happened to the first one."

"What happened to the first one?"

Aaron looked at me, eyes stern. "The mirror."

The small room suddenly felt like a stuffy, overcrowded office. I breathed deeply, inhaling the old, stale air, my body unexpectedly fevered as I sat in the baking heat. Aaron moved to the window, blocking out the early morning light. A single line of sweat ran down his forehead, though he made no attempt to wipe it away. Outside, the storm battled on, hailstones thumping on the boat like marbles rattling around a box. The angry waves smacked against the side of the boat, as though punching, pummelling their way in.

"So…the mirror?" I asked irritably, perplexed by the continuation of the seemingly unstoppable storm. I glanced at my wrist, imagining it slashed open, like Pete's fantastical story. "I doubt a crappy old mirror could destroy a lighthouse."

"The mirror didn't destroy the lighthouse," Aaron replied, bemused.

I rolled my eyes, annoyed. "Get your story straight, mate. You said the first one was destroyed," I snapped. "What? Are you going to tell me there was no lighthouse in 1847? There was no mysterious accident? Listen, I don't have time for this. My dad will be wondering where I am."

Aaron chortled, his eyes brimming with tears. "Your dad doesn't give a rat's arse about you. You're a failure. You know what everyone says at the pub? *He's the fisherman whose son can't fish.* And if you can't fish, what use are you to him? Your mum was worried. Thought you could do with paternal bonding. I heard you've been hanging out with the wrong crowd, that some old guy caught you screwing some bird at the Cleveland cemetery. You know the cemetery was moved, right?"

I shrugged. "So?"

"They used to call it Pumpkin Point. It was swampy, and hard to keep bodies buried. Diggers couldn't dig proper graves and used poles to keep the coffins down. They built the playground over it."

I raised my brows. "The one across from Woolworths?"

"The one and only."

"Morbid," I admitted. "But what does all this have to do with the lighthouse and the mirror? It's hot in here, I'm tired, and I'm sure my dad needs you to gut fish."

Aaron smiled. "I'm sure your dad needs *you* to gut fish. If you could be trusted with a knife."

"I can be trusted with a knife," I muttered, rubbing my tired eyes. "I don't like fishing."

"Child."

Scowling, I slipped from the bunk and paced towards the mirror, staring at my reflection. Gasping, I jumped backwards, tripping over my feet. Rubbing my eyes, I peered at the mirror once more, staring at the dark reddish-brown ligature marks above my Adam's Apple. Aaron raised a mocking brow.

"You can see it, then?"

"See what?" I snapped.

"See what's in the mirror. Or, see what's beyond the mirror."

I turned up my nose, crossing my arms defensively. "I saw nothing. Stop trying to scare me. You're such an arsehole, Aaron. No wonder people say you're a creep. Are you going to tell me about the lighthouse or not? I'd like to fish."

Aaron narrowed his eyes, his expression a mix of bemusement and curiosity. Stomach knotting, I realised he liked having power over others, he liked superiority. He liked to control others and manipulate them. He'd manipulated my dad for years, and the rest of the men on the boat. Now, he was trying to manipulate me. *Well, I won't stand for it!* I thought crossly. *I have a right to be here the same as everyone else.*

"The hexagonal design and use of weatherboards are unique," Aaron continued. "One of the reasons you can't go inside."

"It's closed to the public because it's old and historical."

"No. When the mirror was there, you couldn't go inside. I mean, you physically couldn't go inside. Whoever tried to venture into the lighthouse was turned around for some reason or other, like they'd suddenly remembered to do something they'd forgotten. But when it stormed," Aaron whispered, "and people sought shelter in the lighthouse, whoever was granted access saw the mirror cut their throats, claiming they saw their reflection doing the very same thing. They wrote it in their suicide letters. *The mirror made me do it*. And even though the mirror is gone, is here, people say the ghosts of its victims still haunt the lighthouse. And the mirror itself." He raised his brows, spreading open his palms. "But hey, the life of a lighthouse keeper is lonely, right? Like the life of a fisherman. Anything can happen if you peer long enough into the dark. If you seek shelter from storms, instead of embracing them. And now the mirror is here. Makes you think, huh?"

"Get out of my room."

Aaron rolled his eyes and moved to lean against the doorframe. "You're a kid," he said, "you think science is bollocks and would prefer to put your faith in new-age hippy shit. But this..." he said, gesturing to the mirror, "this is not new-age hippy shit, and it's not something to be laughed off as a joke."

I gave him the finger, gesticulating wildly towards the door. "Get out of here before I tell my dad you're harassing me."

Aaron smirked darkly. "You can't even catch a fish. You won't tell your dad shit. Maybe you should go to sleep."

I slammed the door shut behind him as he slinked off down the narrow hallway, back to the deck of the boat. Inside the room, I breathed angrily, nostrils flaring, taking in the scent of the salty tang of the ocean. I could hear the voices from above, but only faintly, as if they were akin to smells from a spit on a fire, scents blowing in the wind. The reek of the salty air, entwined with my sudden ideas of a pig on a spit, filled my head with images of charred sea octopuses, slow-roasting fish, snapper kebabs. I wondered if any of the men ate fish, considering they smelled like fish themselves. Yawning, I pressed my fingers against my forehead. *Thanks, Mum*, I thought sombrely, *you've made a man out of me now.* And I wanted to be a man. I wanted to be a warrior of the ocean, like the men on deck. I wanted to be muscular and sturdy, my veins pumping with blood ripened by the scent of hooked and bloodied fish. I wanted to feel excitement as my fingers caressed the floppy flesh before I gutted it, warm blood running down my fingers. I wanted to be a real man, a true man, and fearlessly taste the blood in front of my peers as they eagerly cheered me on. Maybe I would be busy enough to tire? Maybe I would sleep? But I was none of those things, and I knew it. The rest of the men knew it. Dad knew it. My mother, at least, clung to a semblance of hope there was still time. Maybe she was wrong.

Outside, the intense storm had not abated. *Must be cluster storms*, I thought, slightly unnerved by the torrent of droplets assaulting the fishing boat. Dad seemed unperturbed, standing against the side of the boat, binoculars around his neck. Pete stood beside him, one foot leaning against a small blue crate, water dripping from his sodden raincoat. Two rats scurried across my feet, and I jumped backwards, bumping into John, an ancient-looking man who leant on a cane for support. Dad liked to refer to him as my surrogate grandfather. Beside him were three plastic containers filled with fish, all dead.

"Hello, lad," John said, standing aside. He tucked his enormously long, grey beard into his belt. "Thought you might have leapt overboard. It's five. Sun will rise in an hour or so. Where've you been?"

"I was in my room. To be honest…" I sighed, pushing my fists into my pockets, "this isn't for me. I hate it. My dad is disappointed in me."

John rolled his eyes. "Your dad? Son, he likes to get under people's skin. He plays cat and mouse, but nothing else. He wants you to succeed. He wants you to do something with your life."

I crossed my arms, huffing in irritation. "Fucker," I said, jerking my thumb towards Aaron. "Told me some bullshit story about the cemetery and the creepy mirror in my room."

"He means well, lad. Listen, I'm gonna head down for a tic. Gotta drain the main vein." He winked. "Will ya hold my line?"

"Sure."

John passed his line to me and hobbled off, his cane tapping against the floorboards. I turned my gaze to the sea. It was now, what Dad had taught me, nautical dawn, and the sun would soon rise. I knew everyone would keep their lines in until civil dawn, when there was enough sunlight to distinguish the horizon from the sea, and the fish would swim back down to the deeper depths of the ocean. Everyone had their flashlights, their lamps, as the sky was still dark. Far off to the left of the sky, patches of yellow and orange poked through the darkness, like knives plunging through paper. I rubbed my tired eyes.

I felt a firm tug on John's line. Pete raised a bushy brow. "I believe you've got something, Lucien."

Brows raised, I held firmly to the line, glancing around for John. I glanced at Pete while wrangling John's line.

"Horrible critters," Pete said icily, eyes steady on the horizon. "Humans, I mean. And stupid."

"Sorry, what?"

"Think they know it all. *When it rains, the fish come out to play?* Give me a break. Although, maybe I am a fish, not human. Bumbling idiots, they are. Everyone are idiots. And they say fishermen are perceptive!"

His condescending tone chilled me to the bone. I wasn't sure if the man was confessing to something, or his words merely sounded menacing because of my own lack of sleep. Either way, I knew I had to get back to my room to see what Aaron was doing.

I glanced over at Dad, silently projecting my fears. I wanted to tell him I was scared. I wanted to tell him how uncomfortable I felt. But I couldn't. He already thought I was nothing more than a snivelling, good-for-nothing child. I knew it. I watched as he bagged and tagged types of fish, his steady hand carefully noting them in the boat's log.

Tired, I leant against the railing, zoning out. I could feel the micro-sleep creeping up my bones, but I pushed it off, determined to stay alert. I knew accidents could happen if I wasn't focussed. I had to stay awake.

"What are you doing?" John snapped his fingers in front of me, snatching the line from my hands.

Nudging me aside, John pulled in a sizable snapper. It twisted and turned as it struggled to break free from the hook, and I watched as John held it to the beckoning sunrise, marvelling at its size.

"Wow-ee!" he exclaimed. Dad and Pete slapped the man on the back, smiles from ear to ear. "You got the catch of the night. The others were throwbacks. Small snapper and the odd kahawai. But this is good.'

Dad finished off his beer. "All mine mooched along, eating anything, and I couldn't nab a keeper."

"Snapper don't see too well in the dark," John said excitedly. "This one must have regained its sight. Caught it in time."

I stood around the men, feigning interest. When the fish was bagged, I slipped away down below. My room was a mess. The sheets on the queen-size bed had been pulled off. The shower was filled with toilet rolls: wet, sticky paper pressed against the tiles like papier-mâché. The small closet door was open, with my clothes strewn out all over the floor. The cushions in the corner lounge were overturned. I looked towards the ornamental mirror, terror flooding my body. The words were written in lipstick, the same bubble-gum pink shade my mother wore.

The mirror made me do it.

Stumbling backwards, I steadied myself on the counter table and looked into the mirror, gasping as my eyes locked onto the pair of boots sticking out from under the blankets on the top bunk. Heart thudding, I slowly turned around, realising the boots belonged to Aaron.

"You know, when I first told Pete to buy the mirror, I didn't know it had come from the old lighthouse," Dad said. He slunk into the room, boots squelching, body dripping water on the floor.

"Someone mentioned it to me at the pub, about the lighthouse, and the mirror came up. An old, half-crazy caretaker told me the story, about people seeking shelter in the lighthouse only to find their own deaths. I thought how curious an object so unassuming could harness so much terror in someone. Sort of like you and fish.'

I stared at Dad, at the tall, bulky man. I had tried so hard not to make a fool of myself in front of his friends. I had kept my jealousy of Aaron to myself for so many years. *The fisherman whose son can't fish.* What a joke! Gasping, I stared into his hard eyes, my jolted mind trying to unravel what he was telling me. I was tired, confused, and all I wanted to do was sleep.

"But you know," Dad continued, "seeking shelter from a storm is not the best thing to do. I thought putting you in this room would persuade you to kill yourself. To slit your wrists with a fishing knife. You'd become so delirious without sleep you'd hook your eyes open, to stay awake in your attempt to impress me. You'd be so tired you'd fall off the boat and drown." He shrugged, spreading his big, bloodied hands. "I read about the stories of the people who claimed the mirror urged them to commit suicide. Perhaps it *was* haunted, like the park. Pete told you about the park, didn't he? About Pumpkin Point?"

I nodded mutely, not bothering to mention it was Aaron, not Pete.

"Oh, it was swampy alright. Men could make careers out of caretaking. All those bodies from the old lighthouse."

I shook my head roughly, clenching and unclenching my fists. "Those were ordinary people," I muttered. "The first people to settle in Cleveland. They were buried there because there was no other cemetery."

Dad raised his finger, signalling my silence. "Ah! They were buried there because they had been inside the lighthouse. They had sought shelter from the storm, in a small, cosy room. They gathered there together, hoping to wait out the storm. They were buried there because they were cursed. Everyone told stories of the haunted lighthouse. Nobody spoke about the mirror," he said, his voice growing louder. "Death by suicide. An unspeakable act, back in the day. You surely wouldn't be going to heaven."

"Now the ghosts haunt the mirror," I mumbled inaudibly, remembering Aaron's words. "Egging them on."

"To join them," Dad said, eyes gleaming. "And it's only a matter of time before you do the same. Because you're weak, you're easily misled, and I never loved you."

He stepped forwards, and I pressed myself against the counter table, eyeing the door.

"Look around you, Lucien. There's no escape."

Dad removed his raincoat and laid it on the floor in front of him. Outside, dribbles of rain splattered on the window like blood, blossoming as the wind pressed against the glass.

"What are you going to do?"

I listened for the distant sounds of the rain, of the thunder, but the air had quietened to a dull lull of restless air and listless bird squawks.

"Tell me what you're going to do, Dad."

Dad stared through the window behind me, looking at the brimming oranges and yellows in the sky. The weather was serene, devoid of all traces of the earlier storm. They'd found shelter at last.

"I've bought another place," he said matter-of-factly, digging his hand into the side pocket of his coat.

"And?"

He pulled out a small pistol, and I recognised it as my mother's Luger. She'd had it ever since Port Arthur, back in 1996. She had moved from Eaglehawk Neck to Brisbane and met Dad a few years later, and they'd had me. But she'd never got rid of the gun, and I was never allowed to touch it.

"Why do you have Mum's gun?"

"This is how it's going to be, Lucien."

He snapped back the safety, his hands steady, eyes pugnacious and stern.

"You can't sleep, you can't fish. You can't even hold or gut a fish. You're an insomniac freak who constantly disappoints me. You know how much you embarrass me, Lucien? How hard it was to get these men out to sea with me? Your entire existence is a joke. Nobody wants to go deep-sea fishing with a man who can't even convince his son to take the trade."

Tears ran down my cheeks as I struggled to hold back my anger. "How could I learn from you?" I shouted hoarsely. "You're busy with Aaron! You told him about me and Sarah! You're a hypocrite!"

Dad paused, thumb on the trigger. "What are you rambling about? Who's Aaron?"

"Don't be an arsehole, Dad! Not now. Not with me. You wish I was Aaron. You wish I loved fishing like he does. Don't lie."

"You're a nutcase, Lucien. Who the fuck is Aaron? One of your make-believe friends? Get a grip."

"Why don't *you* get a grip?" I shouted, my mind whirling. "You think I'm a failure! Why don't you shoot me?"

"Shoot you?"

"Shoot me in the face!"

"In the face?"

I rolled my eyes in infuriation. "You're the one with the gun!"

"You're demented!"

"You're a liar! You're trying to make me think I'm crazy!"

"You *are* crazy!"

A bolt of thunder cracked against the window, and I jumped, dropping the gun. Gasping, I stared at my shaking hands, wondering how it had transferred from Dad to me so fast. *Another micro-sleep, Lucien!* Thunder rattled the room once more. I was a fool to think the storm had abated. Perhaps it had been there all along, and the morning thunder was a wakeup call. A warning. There was no seeking shelter from this storm. I thought back to Aaron's earlier words. "Thunderstorms, rain... Do you ever think they're supposed to wash us away?" he'd asked. "Are they supposed to drench us so we become nothing but a smudge in a Monet masterpiece?" I thought back to our earlier conversation, when he had been trying to intimidate me. "You know, fish are sensitive when it comes to the weather. They sense changes in water pressure. Insects flitter when it's sprinkling, buzzing around, enticing the fish to the surface. They seem to lure the fish, as if they know they're making them more susceptible to being caught. Rain makes humans head indoors, but not here, out in the ocean. Not fish. When it rains, the fish come out to play. And the humans are ready..."

Had I somehow not sensed the change in my dad? Was he the insect luring me, the fish? Was the mirror the web? Had he been lying in wait all this time? Had he been the oncoming storm? The questions flooded my addled mind. There was no-one on the boat I could trust, no place to seek shelter. I was all alone.

"I want to stay down here, keep out of the storm!" I pleaded. "I'm not a fisherman; I can't stand the rain. I can't stand the rotten smell of the fish."

"That's right! You're not a fisherman," he jeered, snatching up the gun. "You should kill yourself."

Aaron moved to stand behind Dad. The rest of the men had

gathered around, telling us both to calm down. Aaron remained still, a presumptuous smirk on his face. For a moment, the clouds dissipated, and I saw Aaron move aside to stand in front of the mirror. I gasped, almost dropping the gun as I saw my reflection.

"Did you bring that here?" I shouted.

"You dragged it here yourself," Dad pleaded. "Half-crazed. We thought you were sleepwalking. Shouting about some haunted lighthouse. That the mirror held ghosts. You're sick. Your mum wanted us to bond so you'd get better."

I pressed my hands to my temples. What was going on? Was Aaron a ghost? Had he been in the lighthouse? "Pete! You said you sliced open your arm after seeing it happen in the mirror!"

Everyone stared at me, mouths open. Thomas covered his mouth in shock, shook his head, and sprinted above deck. Dad slowly shook his head.

"Lucien. Pete killed Aaron in the lighthouse. Then he slit his own throat with a fishing knife. Remember? He left you a note: *The mirror made me do it.*"

"What? I looked over at Pete, at his straight back, his bushy eyebrows. While all the men were soaked, he appeared dry. But that made no sense… Gasping, I watched as Aaron stepped backwards and passed through the mirror, disappearing. The sky was pink and clear.

Pressing the gun to my head, I pulled the trigger.

Story Publishing History

All stories are copyright Claire Fitzpatrick.

"Madeline" *Midnight Echo magazine Issue 13 2018;* reprinted in *Dead Of Night: The Best Of Midnight Echo* 2016

"Eat" *Breach magazine, Issue 2* 2017

"Mechanical Garden" *Aphelion: The Webzine of Science Fiction and Fantasy, April 2018*

"The Jacaranda House" *Teleport magazine November Issue 2017*

"Transplant" Original to this collection

"The Eagle" Excerpt published as 'The Bird Woman' in *A Parliament Of Vowels, 2017;* published in full in *Disturbed Digest, June 2018*

"Scarab" *Breach magazine, Issue 7* 2018

"Senses" *The Horror Zine Ghost Stories* 2018

"The Dog" First Place, *University of Queensland Writers' Club Competition,* 2016

"The Town Hall" *Breach magazine, Issue 5* 2017

"Metamorphosis" *Midnight Echo, Issue 13, 2018*

"Happy Birthday, Ebony" First Place *UQ Writers' Club Competition 2017;* First published in *A Parliament Of Vowels* anthology, 2017

"Synthetic" *Breach magazine Issue 4 2017;* Republished in *Phantaxis Magazine 7 2017*

"Andromeda" *Nebula Rift magazine, Vol. 4 No.3 2014*

"The Perfect Son" Original to this collection

"Thorne House" *Tricksters Treats, #1 2017*

"Deep-sea Fishing" Shelter From The Storm 2018